EYE
of the
SUN

DON'T MISS THE BEGINNING OF THE STORY.

EYE of the MOON

DIANNE HOFMEYR

EYE
of the
SUN

Aladdin

NEW YORK   LONDON   TORONTO   SYDNEY

ALADDIN

An imprint of Simon & Schuster Children's Publishing Division
1230 Avenue of the Americas, New York, NY 10020
First Aladdin paperback edition July 2011
Copyright © 2008 by Dianne Hofmeyr
Originally published in Great Britain in 2008 by Simon & Schuster UK Ltd, a CBS company.
Published by arrangement with Simon & Schuster UK Ltd.
All rights reserved, including the right of reproduction in whole or in part in any form.
ALADDIN is a trademark of Simon & Schuster, Inc.,
and related logo is a registered trademark of Simon & Schuster, Inc.
For information about special discounts for bulk purchases, please contact Simon & Schuster
Special Sales at 1-866-506-1949 or business@simonandschuster.com.
The Simon & Schuster Speakers Bureau can bring authors to your live event.
For more information or to book an event contact the Simon & Schuster Speakers Bureau
at 1-866-248-3049 or visit our website at www.simonspeakers.com.
Designed by Ann Zeak and Irene Metaxatos
The text of this book was set in Centaur MT.
Manufactured in the United States of America 0611 OFF
2 4 6 8 10 9 7 5 3 1
Library of Congress Control Number 2010940168
ISBN 978-1-4424-1186-9
ISBN 978-1-4424-1187-6 (eBook)

For Phillip

Prologue

✦ ✕ ✦ ✕ ✦ ✕ ✦ ✕ ✦

An owl swoops down. There's a strangled screech followed by an uneasy silence.

The sounds and rustlings of the night have set his imagination running. He feels that at any moment something will loom up out of the shadows. His skin prickles. His heart beats faster.

Who's there? he wants to call out. But there's nothing except the hoarse bark of a dog in the distance and the dry smell of dust in the air. Now a more pungent odor pinches his nose. Perhaps a desert fox is prowling for scraps of food at the offering altars.

He looks about uneasily.

The towering statue of his father glares down in the moonlight. His stony eyes are narrowed and unblinking. The edges of his gigantic nostrils flare. The carved line of his lips seems to sneer. Behind him the Temple of Amun is silent and secretive. Along its walls, carved creatures with curved claws, jagged snouts, and fierce fangs wait silently to pounce. And throats and chests of enemies are forever still as they wait for the arrows that are directed at their stone hearts.

All are frozen into silence by the bloodless moon.

The paving stones are still warm under his feet. His fingers feel for the comfort of the giant scarab beetle. The stone has been polished by the touch of many hands.

He feels exposed here next to the moon-splintered water of the Sacred Lake. This is the wrong place to have agreed to meet his brother. The inner sanctum would've been safer. In the inner sanctum the gods would surely protect the son of a king against the dark evils of the night.

It's strange to be back in Thebes. After the emptiness of the desert, with its far horizon and the wide stretches of river, his eyes aren't used to the boundaries set by the stone walls that anchor Thebes to the Great River.

And it's strange not to have returned to the palace.

No one knows he has returned. He has kept his identity secret. At all costs he has to speak to his brother first. He needs his brother's protection.

A sense of something behind him—an imperceptible movement—makes him turn.

He sees a face made pale by the moonlight. The hand clutches an object that glints.

In the moonlight the dagger is sharp and hard and unforgiving.

"You!" The word is more breath than sound.

The blade finds the soft spot just below his ribs and angles upward, seeking his heart. Two quick thrusts. Hard and brutal.

The blows make him gasp with their suddenness. No words are possible now. The blade is swiftly withdrawn.

He sees the hand that clutches the hilt. He knows it well. It's unmistakable. He looks down and sees the huge dark stain seeping through his tunic. He slams his fist against it. Presses harshly with both hands against his chest. As if in pushing he will stop his life from flowing from his body. But he knows it's too late.

He looks into the narrowed eyes of the face in front of him and sees the same answer in them. It's too late.

Someone calls his brother's name. Over and over. A voice that's surely not his own. It threads and weaves through the darkness.

Around him the night pants like a savage creature. The sky expands. The stars reel. His heart thrums in his head louder and louder . . . until he hears nothing but the sound exploding inside him.

PART ONE

1

THE ENCOUNTER

Thebes is the color of chalk—a mixture of sand swirling up from the desert and dust billowing down from the ancient limestone mountains. It sifts down over the city like fine bread flour. And this morning hordes of people with handcarts and donkeys pushing their way through the narrow streets were kicking up even more dust than usual.

I felt a shiver of excitement. This was going to be

the best market ever. Traders were coming from far-off Syria with exotic oils, woven cloths, spices, and nuggets of precious stone as large as duck eggs.

It didn't help that there was no ferryman waiting on the west bank of the Great River. The crowd was restless. Children squalled and mothers scolded. I pulled the rough cloak around my head and hoped no one would recognize me.

When a boat finally came, the crush was so great that an old woman fell from the quayside and disappeared under the water.

"She's not coming up! Quickly, do something!"

"Perhaps a crocodile's got her!"

"Oi! You! If a crocodile's got her, *you* won't be coming back either," someone shouted as a boy teetered on the edge of the ferry, ready to jump in after her.

He dived all the same and came up dragging the woman. They were hauled back onto the ferry. People laughed and teased as they picked off strands of waterweed from the old woman's hair and tunic.

All this took time. Eventually on the east bank, I was carried along by a surge of people like a bit of debris swept down by the flood. Men, women, large and small, old and young, all mingled with loud shrieks and yelps as carts were overturned, a child fell, and a dog was trodden underfoot. In the midst of this some geese escaped their cages and were honking and hissing and snapping at passing feet.

A pestilence of flies! My tunic hem was dragging in the dirt, and through some fresh donkey droppings as well.

There was a loud curse behind me. "Oi! Mind where you're going, stupid girl!"

I had barely time to save myself from falling under the wheels of a handcart piled high with onions and leeks, when someone held out a hand to steady me.

"Watch out! They'll flatten you as quickly as oxen trampling through barley," he shouted over the noise of the geese. "Come to the side of the road. You're limping."

I glanced at the boy as he examined my foot. He looked familiar.

"Your sandals are ridiculous with those upturned tips! No wonder you tripped! You need strong leather sandals on market day!" He pressed around my ankle.

"Ouch! That hurt!" I snapped at him.

"It's only twisted. But it needs to be bound."

I pulled away and tried to stand. "I'm fine, thank you!"

"You're not! Sit down. I'll bind it for you."

I looked back at him. Smooth, freshly shaved cheeks. No formal wig. His hair falling in damp tendrils against his neck. "Aren't you the boy who saved the old woman?"

He shrugged. "Saving old women or princesses, it's all the same to me!"

"Princesses?"

He raised a dark eyebrow and grinned at me. "Your rough cloak doesn't fool me. I can see by your fine linen tunic you're no country girl come to town on market day. You don't belong here, do you?"

I glanced quickly over my shoulder in case anyone had overheard.

"Don't look so dismayed. Your secret won't be told. It's safe with me."

"I'm . . ." I left off and brushed his hand from my foot, eager to get away. He jumped up just as abruptly and pulled me against his chest.

"Huh?" I gave him a sharp jab with my elbow. "What do you think you're doing? Let go of me!"

"I will, as soon as that donkey has passed. You

almost got yourself knocked down again. Now sit calmly while I bandage your foot." He grinned at me. "I know what I'm doing. This isn't the first time I've done this. Trust me."

He drew a dagger from his girdle, stuck its point into the linen of his tunic, and deftly tore a strip from the hem. Then he removed my sandal and began winding the strip firmly under my foot and around my ankle. I eyed him as he worked. His hands were quick and seemed practiced at bandaging. His forearms were crisscrossed with pale scars, and the fingers of his right hand looked as if they'd once been badly broken. He was about the age of my brother. About fifteen or sixteen.

He glanced up and caught my look.

I felt my face grow hot.

He smiled with perfect even teeth. "You're not from Thebes, are you?"

"How do you know?"

"The stupid upturned sandals. The braided style of your wig. Are you Syrian?"

I shook my head.

"Perhaps from Tyre, or Byblos, or even Kadesh. You're not Nubian."

I shook my head again.

"From where, then?"

"What's it to you? You ask too many questions."

He laughed, released my foot, and stood up quickly. "There. The way is clear now." He bowed slightly as if giving me permission to leave.

"Clear?" I turned to look at the people brushing past us, almost wishing another trail of donkeys could delay me. "I'm from Mitanni. The people here call it Naharin. But I prefer its real name."

"From Naharin?"

"*Mitanni.*"

He inclined his head and smiled. "So you *are* a princess! A princess sent from Mitanni to Thebes as a gift to the king."

"I'm *not* a princess!"

"But you *are* from the palace?"

I glanced sharply at him. "What makes you say that?"

"Why else are you wearing a peasant's wrap over a fine linen tunic? You've sneaked out and you don't want anyone to recognize you. But mysterious girls with cat tattoos are easy to recognize."

"Cat tattoos?" I snatched at my cloak. I'd forgotten the tattoo on my shoulder. A blush crept up my neck. This boy was a flirt. Yet even though I knew he was flirting, I was still charmed.

"I have to hurry," I said quickly.

"Go, then, Little Cat Girl."

"That's not my proper name."

He smiled and held my eyes. "Beware of carts and donkeys!"

And boys with dark, flirting eyes, I almost blurted out. But he turned before I could say anything and slipped into the crowd and disappeared.

My sandals were nowhere to be seen. Standing barefoot in the dust, I really did feel like a proper country girl. A pestilence of flies! I'd have to walk barefoot through the muck, and my ankle would slow me down. The sun was stinging hot. And now I was late. And Kiya would be impatient for her length of cloth.

"Fine linen, woven with gold thread, with tasseled edges and a pattern of turquoise beads caught into it—is what I want, Ta-Miu," she'd said.

"How can you be sure I'll find such cloth?"

"The traders are from Syria. Everything at the market will be wonderful." She had sighed heavily. "I wish I could go with you."

"You can't, and that's that! It's too dangerous."

"I promise to behave. Please, Ta-Miu, let me go."

But all her flouncing and flopping about on her bed hadn't convinced me. I couldn't risk it. Kiya was too impulsive. She'd have drawn attention to us.

When she'd seen that nothing would make me change my mind, she'd pouted and said, "Bring wool cloth as well."

"Wool? This isn't the Khābūr Mountains, Kiya. We don't need wool here."

"It's not the wool I need but the comfort of it. I miss the feel of it beneath my fingers. Three years in Thebes haven't cured me of longing for things that remind me of home."

I had sighed. Sometimes Kiya—Princess Tadukhepa to others, but Kiya always to me—seemed such a child. How would she ever cope with her position as wife to the new king?

By the time I eventually reached the stalls, the market was seething with people. Over the stench of donkey droppings came aromas of sizzling goat meat and perfumed wafts of cinnamon, caraway, coriander, saffron, mint, thyme, and every other conceivable herb and spice. Hawks whirled overhead trying to snap up entrails, and were shooed off by angry stallholders. The hawks' screeches added confusion to the sound of foreign tongues, donkeys braying, voices arguing over goods, and volleys of slaps and curses as tempers flew and the day grew more and more stifling.

I kept a lookout for the boy. But in the mass of people pushing me this way and that, all I could do was edge my way forward and curse myself for not asking his name. He had come close to guessing mine. Little Cat Girl, he'd called me.

In a city as large as Thebes, I'd probably never lay eyes on him again. Who was to say he was even Theban? He might've been passing through for market day and be gone by tomorrow and on his way to another place.

I came to a stall piled high with woven fabric and trimmings, and I rifled through them. When I saw a cloth that I thought would make Kiya happy, I bargained as hard as I could and shrugged off others who tried to grasp it from me. Eventually a small sachet of ten orange carnelians tipped into the trader's hand did the trick. With the cloth firmly bundled under my arm, I shouldered my way through the crowds and came to a space where I could right my clothing and breathe freely again.

The cloth was woven with a pattern of fine red thread and was hung with tassels but had no beads of turquoise or gold. Not exactly what Kiya had asked for, but perhaps I could sew on some beads. I knew why she had to have something unusual and exotic for the banquet. This was the first proper gathering of all the royal wives since Nefertiti's marriage to Amenhotep the Younger. Kiya, being the youngest of all his foreign wives, wanted to make an impression.

Suddenly someone grabbed me around the waist and held a hand over my mouth. There was a whisper at my ear. "It's only me, Little Cat Girl!"

I spun around. "Are you following me?" I snapped.

"Only for your protection."

"Well, *don't!* I don't need your protection! I've traveled across the deserts of Syria on my own."

He smiled knowingly. "Not entirely on your own. You were accompanied by hordes of fierce horsemen as protectors."

I looked over my shoulder. "You think you know everything. Keep your voice down!" I urged.

"In this hubbub no one will hear us. Here. These

are yours." He held up my sandals with a smile that seemed to mock the upturned toe. "I found them alongside the road. The market is thirsty work. I know a place where we can get something to drink. Come."

He gripped my arm and guided me firmly down a tangle of narrow streets into a small alleyway. At the end of it I could see a glint of green as the river flowed by. An old man was sitting in a dark doorway. The boy handed him a bag of dates. In return the man poured out two horn cupfuls of pomegranate juice and pushed two honey cakes toward us.

The juice was bitter but cool. I was thirsty. The boy gulped his and was left with a pink mustache. It was difficult not to smile.

"I can't stay long," I said. "Tadukhepa is waiting."

"Tadukhepa?"

"Princess Tadukhepa . . . my mistress." I wiped the crumbs of honey cake from my lips. "Although she's three years younger than I."

"The *real* princess!" His eyes glinted in the shadowy light. "So I was right! You traveled from Mitanni with a princess. You *did* have fierce horsemen as your protectors. The finest and most valiant of horsemen. The Mitannians are famous for the way they train horses. Even the Hittites are jealous of them. And now you live at the palace here in Thebes."

"Are you asking or telling?"

"You don't have to be secretive. I can keep secrets."

"Perhaps another time. I must hurry now."

"Meet me again. Here tomorrow at the same time?"

Hmm. No "please" or "will you" from this boy. I shrugged. "Perhaps."

"Perhaps is good enough! Hurry, then, before you're missed. You've a banquet to attend."

I gave him a sharp glance. "How do you know?"

He smiled. "In Thebes it's not only dust that fills the air."

I took the less crowded route back to the river. Next to the new Southern Opet Temple a smell of myrrh drifted in the air. In the sunlight slanting through the columns, I caught sight of priests making offerings before the altars. They swung censers and mumbled incantations that echoed against the shining blocks of stone and newly carved papyrus-shaped columns.

Apart from the priests, there was no one. Not even the temple cleaning women, or the urchin boys who usually hung about pelting one another with pebbles and pestering people for a loaf of bread.

I hurried as quickly as my ankle would allow down the avenue of sphinxes that guarded the east and the west horizons between the Southern Opet Temple and the Temple of Amun. Along the way I stopped to touch the seventeenth lioness facing east. She was the one I always touched, the one with the strange expression that made her look wiser than the rest. Her body was warm under my hand, as if power were trapped in her stone lion muscles.

"So . . . what do you think about this boy?" I asked.

Her expression remained as wise as ever.

Then I hurried on down the long avenue. And as I passed through the shadows cast by the lions, with bands of sunlight between them, I felt I was zithering across the strings of a giant lyre. An inaudible vibration seemed to float upward. My feet were as light as air. My heart sang.

2

THE HEART SCARAB

In the palace gardens I stopped to bathe my ankle in a rill of water. The sound of angry voices and footsteps coming closer on the gravel pathway made me pause in the middle of undoing the bandage around my ankle. The voices came from behind some pillars on the other side of a colonnade.

"It has to be done!" a girl's voice spat.

"It's too soon!" a man answered back.

"It's never too soon. I *must* be obeyed."

"But this is not the way. You'll upset them."

"I *must* have rules."

"There's no point in making rules just for the purpose of making them."

"Rules give me power."

I held myself quiet in my hiding place that was not a true hiding place at all. If they'd chosen to walk this way, I'd immediately have been spotted. But there was nothing to be done now except sit on the step and listen.

"Did you learn nothing from Queen Tiy?"

"Like what?"

"Queen Tiy charmed people to do as she wished *without* laying down laws that would upset them."

"I'm *not* his mother."

"But you *are* the queen now. Your youth and beauty will draw people to your side. You don't have to fight for attention."

Queen? Was this Nefertiti on the other side of the colonnade?

"Take heed of how Queen Tiy governed," the man's voice went on. "She was a woman of great passion, just like you. Yet she managed an entire palace to do her bidding. She had her own perfumery. Her own royal barge. A lake built for her pleasure. Her own temple erected as far away as Abu Island on the edge of Nubia."

"Tchh! Queen Tiy this! Queen Tiy that! I'm sick of her name!"

"But she earned respect."

"It's your fault, Wosret."

I held myself rigid. Wosret? So the man Nefertiti was speaking to was the highest of high priests.

"My fault?"

"You said my husband had to keep his father's wives. It could have ended"—I heard Nefertiti snap her fingers—"if you'd changed the rule. Then I would have been the first and *only* wife."

"I can't change tradition. Kings of Egypt have always had many royal wives. It shows their enemies how powerful they are. But kings of Egypt have one advantage. Not military power . . . but *gold*. The greatest of foreign kings are desperate for Egypt's gold. They are prepared to beg for it. The king gives gold but leaves them wanting more. They exchange gifts, not blows. In return for gold the foreign kings give their daughters—foreign princesses with dowries and attendants that make the king of Egypt even richer and more powerful. King Amenhotep employed personal ambassadors to find him the very best wives. The palace is full of the most beautiful daughters of the most powerful kings. It's a brotherhood between the great kings. It needs to stay this way."

"I don't care. I want to be the king's only wife. Now I have to contend with that young girl from Naharin . . . Princess Tadukhepa."

Tadukhepa? Kiya? I bit my lip. What would Nefertiti say about Kiya?

"Princess Tadukhepa is not a rival. She's a child. As queen you *must* care about what people think of your husband. Having many wives is a sign of power, not only to foreign kings but to the people of Egypt as well. What would they think if their new king had only one wife?"

"It's none of their business," Nefertiti snapped.

"But it's *mine.* Don't you understand? I want you to be supreme. I'm here to guide you. Trust me. If the palace wives want to enjoy a little luxury, what does it matter? Let them get on with it. Let them play their silly games of dressing up. You are superior."

"I don't need your *lectures,* Wosret!"

"I do it for your own good. Fourteen is very young

to be ruling a country as powerful as Egypt. *Someone* must guide you."

"I don't need guidance. I'm the first royal wife. And the first royal wife must be listened to and obeyed."

I craned my neck to get a better view. Yes, it was definitely Nefertiti standing there in the sunlight. Even though she wore no crown or royal headdress, I could tell by her long neck and the way she held her head. And the man, with his clean-shaved head, was definitely the highest of high priests, Wosret.

Who else would have the courage to tell Nefertiti what she could or could not do?

"Take my advice. Make sure you give him a child soon."

"A child? Never!"

I could hear the shock in her voice.

"All you have to do is produce a son and you'll be the darling of all Egypt."

"I don't want a baby. I don't want my stomach swollen, or the sickness that comes with it, or *anything* to do with babies!" I heard her stamp her foot. "You lied to me, Wosret. You said I had to marry Amenhotep. You didn't say anything about having children. I'm not going to stumble around like an ox while the foreign princesses flit around like tiny dragonflies."

"Your beauty is beyond any in the land."

"What if the baby's a girl?"

"It won't be a girl. But if it is, you must have another, until a boy is born."

"Enough! I'm not listening anymore."

The priest sighed heavily. "It's for your own good. You and I want the same. I want you to be the most brilliant and powerful queen Egypt has *ever* known. Your name must be written up in stone."

"It will be!"

"Then listen. Tread carefully. *Mold* people to your wishes. Don't be in such a hurry. Stealth is needed. Believe me, I know! A soft paw treads better than one with claws unsheathed. Don't waste your time making rules for princesses. Your husband, Amenhotep, is young. Spend your time more profitably guiding him. As queen there are facts you must know. Territorial disputes. Cattle and herd numbers. Reservoirs and food supply. Records of rainfall. Levels of the Great River during its flood. Crop production."

"Don't be ridiculous. I'm a *queen*, not a farmer!

My chief vizier can look after those matters."

"Documents need your seal to be authentic and binding. Tax records, storehouse receipts, crop assessments, and agricultural statistics all need your seal. You're supposed to read the reports."

"That's too boring! You can't expect me to read them!"

"You won't have to. I'll read them. You'll only have to make your seal. Trust me! Family members, particularly those who hold a claim to the throne, can *never* be trusted. I'll be your adviser. Your *only* adviser."

Trust Wosret? Never! I knew him too well. I jumped up. There was a small tinkling sound at my feet. A piece of glass lay on the stone step. It could only have fallen from the bandage.

Wosret's voice broke off. "What was that?"

I stood as still as a stone pillar.

"Who knows? It could've been a myriad of things. A cricket chirping. The water in a rill. A servant dropping something."

"Our discussions are secret. They mustn't be overheard. Come, it's nearly time for the banquet. I urge you, Nefertiti, take my advice, and do not . . ." His voice trailed off as they moved away and disappeared down the colonnade. Their sandals made crunching sounds as they walked.

Only when they'd gone did I dare pick up the piece of glass. I sat with my feet dangling in the rill of water and held the glass in the palm of my hand. It caught the light of the setting sun and glinted back at me. A scarab beetle. Symbol of the god Khepera. The creator god who rolled the sun across the sky. It was the kind of amulet that was layered into a mummy's bandages to bring the real heart back to life in the afterlife.

There was a hole between the front feelers so it could be worn as a charm. Its body was of plain blue glass, but the wings had been made with inlaid slices of colored green and purple glass that mirrored the luster on a real scarab beetle.

I rubbed my thumb slowly across it. First Wosret and Nefertiti . . . and now this. How had it got between the wraps of bandage on my foot? There was only one person who could have put it there. But why?

I felt the feathery tickle of tiny fish swimming past my feet in the rill. The air was flinty with the smell of hot wet stone. In the west the tall cypress trees stood like dark statues against a sky the color of pomegranate juice, and the last red gash of sunset shone through the dip in the mountains of the desert—the Gap of Abydos. I had to hurry to prepare for the banquet.

There was no time for me to catch up with my thoughts.

3

KIYA'S QUARTERS

Kiya was in her chambers sitting in the middle of her rumpled bed, with clothes strewn about her. She was earnestly watching her pet chameleon crawl along her hand toward a dead fly balanced on her forearm. Lined up on the bed was a collection of more dead flies and beetles.

She jumped up as she saw me, and sent the insects scattering. "I thought you'd never come! What have you brought?"

"Careful, Kiya." I guided the chameleon from her hand onto a branch inside a special wicker cage.

She grabbed me by the shoulders. "Where have you been, Ta-Miu? I've been waiting and waiting. Why are your cheeks so pink?"

It was hard to keep things secret from Kiya. I'd planned to make her drag the news from me, but now that I was with her, the words tripped off my tongue. "An old woman fell into the river and had to be pulled out. I injured my foot. A boy helped me. And I overheard an interesting conversation in the palace courtyard."

"Is that all? But what about the market? What was it like? Did you find the cloth? And the people? Were there lots of people?"

"Hundreds." I tossed my head and laughed at her eagerness. "Maybe even thousands!"

"And acrobats and fire-eaters?"

I nodded. "And talking monkeys, too!"

"Talking monkeys?"

"I'm just teasing."

Kiya sighed heavily as she sank back onto her rumpled bed and flicked the dead flies away with quick, angry movements. "I knew I should've gone with you. I could've been disguised as well."

"My disguise wasn't enough."

"What?" Her eyebrows shot upward. "You mean you were noticed?"

"Not exactly."

"What, then?"

"I met someone."

Kiya swiveled around to face me. "Who?"

"A boy."

"A boy? The one who helped you? So *that's* why your cheeks are pink! Who is he?"

"I don't know his name."

"What was he like? Egyptian or foreign?"

I shook the cloth so that its ends floated up into the air to distract her. "Look what I found."

She grabbed hold of it and lifted the gossamer-fine length up against the lamplight and ruffled the threaded tassels. "Perfect! Nefertiti will wish *she'd* been at the market."

I held out the glass scarab. "And I found this."

"Found it?"

I shrugged. "The boy gave it to me."

"The mysterious boy!" Her eyes flashed with excitement. "What a fine gift." She cradled the scarab in her hands and drew the lamp nearer. "It must have cost him dearly. Look closely. It's no ordinary glass scarab. Look at the brilliance on the wings. He must be *very* rich. Perhaps he's a foreign prince come to find an Egyptian bride."

"Foreign princes don't search for their own brides. And he didn't really give it to me. I found it between the bindings he'd wound around my foot. I'm not sure he meant for me to have it."

"Of course he did, Ta-Miu. He was just too shy to give it to you directly." She untied a thick rope of twisted gold from around her neck, threaded the scarab onto it, and retied it around my neck. "You must make a sacred ritual to bring out its magical power. That way you will be truly blessed whenever you wear it. Is he handsome?"

"Perhaps."

She gave me a quick look. "More handsome than Tuthmosis?"

"I can't say." The glass scarab lay coolly against my skin, alongside the ankh key Tuthmosis had given me the night he'd escaped Thebes. I'd arranged a boat for him but hadn't laid eyes on him since. It was said he'd been captured by a tribe of fierce Medjay somewhere in the desert.

Kiya laughed. "Remember how the serving girls tagged behind him and made flower wreaths for him? He was truly handsome, with his dark lashes and strange blue eyes and broad shoulders."

I nodded. Tuthmosis had intrigued us both when we'd first arrived at the palace. We'd scarcely looked at the younger brother, Amenhotep, who'd been too busy making model reed boats and floating them in the canals. Despite Tuthmosis's leg injury and the way his leg dragged, he had seemed handsome. The hooded falcon he'd carried on his wrist had made him even more alluring. Kiya and I had followed him about, as starry-eyed as the serving girls. But it was the girl, Isikara, he'd escaped with, leaving us behind.

I shrugged. "The serving girls had no claim on him. It was you, Kiya, who was to be his wife."

"Where do you think Tuthmosis is now?"

"I wish we knew." I listened to the clear liquid notes of Kiya's pet golden oriole as it sang from its cage next to her bed.

"Do you think he's truly captured? I can't bear the thought of him being a prisoner in a Medjay camp in the deserts of Nubia. And now I'm betrothed to his brother, Amenhotep the Younger." She gave a deep sigh. "And I don't want to be."

I glanced across at her. By the light of the oil lamps, her face, with its slightly upturned nose, was very young- and innocent-looking. "Amenhotep will treat you kindly. And I'll be here with you."

"It's not Amenhotep I worry about. It's Nefertiti."

I shook my head. "It's *Wosret* you should worry about. Wosret wanted to get rid of Tuthmosis. He would have killed him if Tuthmosis hadn't escaped. Wosret can't be trusted. Not *ever!* We must watch out for him."

I glanced at the serving girls, who were carrying urns of water and preparing the oils and unguents for Kiya's bath, and I dropped my voice. "Listen to what I heard Wosret say to Nefertiti this afternoon. . . ."

While I sprinkled the new cloth with rose water to get rid of the smell of the trader's rags and chase off any stray fleas, .I told Kiya what I'd overheard between Wosret and Nefertiti.

An attendant fidgeted next to Kiya. "You'll be late, Princess Tadukhepa. We need to pin and arrange your wig now."

Kiya pulled a small face and picked up a bronze

mirror from between the ivory combs and brushes and glass vials of perfumes that stood on a table. Two girls began to arrange the braids of her wig. She glanced at me in the mirror, the golden lamplight flickering over her earnest expression. "What do you suppose they were planning?"

I shrugged. "Wosret never *plans*. He only *plots*! Tonight we must be vigilant."

"Let's hurry, then!" She swung around to face me. "You must help me, Ta-Miu. Tonight I must show everyone that a princess from Mitanni can stand up to an Egyptian queen. I'll wear the cloth you bought tied in place around my waist with an emerald brooch, and I'll wear my largest gold disk earrings as well."

I laughed. "You'll dazzle them like a jewel."

Kiya wrinkled her nose. "It's hard to be a jewel when Nefertiti herself is so flawless."

"Be brave now! You forget she's half Mitannian, even though she claims to be entirely Egyptian now that she's the first royal wife."

Kiya grinned. "Maybe that's why she dislikes me so much."

NEFERTITI

The evening air drew out heavy perfumes of fig and musk rose, and trumpets of moon-flower with moths circling about them gave off a scent of sweet honey as Kiya and I set out.

For every step of the way, our feet were guided by lights. Right around the immense lake built for Queen Tiy, snail shells filled with citron-scented oil lined the paths. And tiny papyrus floats, each burning with oil, drifted across the surface of the lake. It seemed Nut, the goddess of the sky, had allowed an entire armful of stars to topple to Earth. Yet the sky still held myriads more that reflected back a lake of stars above us.

A shiver of anticipation ran through me. What was more exciting than a banquet given by a new queen?

We passed through the gateway of the Great Hall, with its huge cedar posts and whispering flags. Long low tables were arranged around three sides of the Great Hall. Gold goblets and platters of silver and glass glinted in the light of flares. Piles of grapes, apricots, plums, and pomegranates lay glistening like brilliant jewels on bronze trays. To one side a group of Syrian slaves played lyres, while at the far end some girls played harps and double flutes.

As we entered, attendants hung flower wreaths around our necks and then offered us sweet-smelling oils from fine alabaster jars. We touched the oil to our foreheads and wrists and took fragrant wax cones and placed them on our heads. More and more royal wives entered the Great Hall, trailed by servants and pet monkeys and cats on long leads.

Kiya nudged me. "I could have brought my pet chameleon."

"And have it eaten by a monkey?"

We sat on low stools while serving girls brought platters of steaming fish and trussed fowl. From woven trays the servants offered rolled durum wheat, flavored with apricots, pine kernels, and rose water. Then a team of eight men staggered forward with a wooden board hoisted up on their shoulders that held an oryx gazelle, honey-glazed and roasted, complete with its long, dark horns.

Attendants refilled our goblets with wine, and the royal sealer of wine drew our attention to the names of the wine. Names such as Star of Horus and Height of Heaven, and an ancient Chassut that was as dark and thick and red as blood and marked three times good.

"Just a few sips!" I added water to Kiya's so that it was more pale pink than red.

"To us!" she cheered, and held her goblet up and gave it a chink against mine. "These are my favorites." She sighed as she took up handfuls of honeyed figs stuffed with pistachios.

There was no sign of Nefertiti. The evening became rowdier. Cats and monkeys bounded about, snarling and hissing and chasing one another, and snatching food from passing trays while their leads twined around everyone's legs.

Kiya made a face. "What's taking her so long?"

A flurry of music finally announced Nefertiti. She entered the Great Hall with a scowling Wosret trailing behind her.

What an entrance she made! Libyan slaves with stiff feathers poking up from their short hair carried gigantic fans made of ostrich plumes, and two Nubian slaves led young cheetahs snarling and hissing alongside them. Another slave led a small giraffe by a red silken cord—its legs so long and spindly, it looked scarcely old enough to have been weaned from its mother.

They were followed by a trail of handmaidens and serving girls too numerous to count. The entire Great Hall echoed with the sound of sandals slapping against stone and the *chink, chink, chink* of bracelets and earrings and the susurration of floor-sweeping robes and girls' whispers and stifled giggles mixing here and there with a sharp rebuke from an older handmaiden.

All eyes were captivated.

"She knows how to make an entrance!"

"She's a *child*! I'd forgotten how young she is!"

"But with the figure of a woman! What would I give for a waist like that?"

"What jewels! Have you ever seen anything like them?"

"They say she spends like mad!"

"Look at her cheekbones. Sharp enough to fit into the cup of your hand. Some say her mother was a princess from Naharin."

Wosret held his hand up for silence. His dark lizard eyes darted quickly from side to side. He bowed, then held up Nefertiti's hand. "Great First Royal Wife Nefertiti, may she live, prosper, and be happy forever!"

Everyone answered back, "Great First Royal Wife Nefertiti, may she live, prosper, and be happy forever!"

She was wearing the magnificent vulture crown that proclaimed her the foremost lady of most royal of wives. With its tall ostrich plumes and gold Aten sun disks, it made her taller than anyone else in the Great Hall. The gold wings of the vulture goddess swept past her brows and across her cheekbones and gleamed with jewels. And hanging from her ears were the gold striking cobras of the cobra goddess, protector of pharaohs. Their red ruby eyes flared in the lamplight. A gold broad collar stretched right from the base of her long neck to the edge of her shoulders and dipped across her breasts. Beneath that her fine tunic fell to the floor.

Wosret give her a dark look as she turned to him with a smile and nodded almost playfully. Then she swept an imperious glance around, meeting the eyes of every woman in the front row. Despite being younger than most, she forced them by the sheer intensity of her gaze to lower their eyes first, and refused to glance at the next person until they did so.

When it was Kiya's turn, Nefertiti inclined her head. "Ah, the girl from Naharin. Is it not beyond your bedtime?"

I gripped Kiya's tunic to keep her from answering impulsively, knowing full well she was only two years younger than Nefertiti.

But I needn't have worried. With all the breeding of her royal Mitanni background, Kiya managed a smile and bowed low with both her hands stretched up in obeisance. "My queen, you do me great honor to single me out."

I was proud of her.

A look of annoyance crossed Nefertiti's face. Then her eyes swept quickly on, ignoring mine as if to suggest she'd already lost interest. "It seems everyone is here!" She inclined her head slightly toward Wosret. I was close enough to hear her murmur, "Now you may leave."

Wosret bowed but stood firm. "I prefer to stay."

She smiled at him. "Stay, then, but step backward." She stepped in front of him so he couldn't direct her. I noticed a flash of anger pass across his face.

"I, Nefertiti, the embodiment of the goddess Tefnut, who showers Egypt with rain and kindness, bring you greetings from my husband, your king, Amenhotep the Younger. He hopes you have enjoyed the banquet."

I marveled at her composure. She was standing in front of at least five hundred royal wives and handmaidens, many of them much older than herself, yet there was no quaver in her voice. Then I saw her neck stiffen. Maybe it was the weight of the crown, or perhaps, after all, she was trying to give herself courage.

"I wish to announce new rules of conduct for royal wives. These will replace all those that have gone before."

There was an intake of breath. Everyone leaned forward to hear what she would say next. The palace was governed by what Queen Tiy had put in place. It wasn't possible that rules *could* change. Until her death the palace had been in perfect harmony for thirty years. There was never any trouble between wives except for an occasional flare-up due more to moon phases than to true jealousy.

To make sure her point was taken, Nefertiti paused and looked around.

I saw Wosret reach out and try to touch her arm, but with a small movement she created a distance between them.

"We need to curb expenses."

Kiya turned to glance at me. The court of Egypt was wealthy. We knew about Egypt's gold. It was gold that had enticed Kiya's father to send her to Egypt.

Nefertiti gestured to her scribe, who was sitting cross-legged beside her, writing a record of the proceedings on a scroll. He handed her a separate roll of papyrus. She began reading.

"The new rules are as follows. One. The height of any headdress worn by ladies of the palace may be no higher than a cone of wax."

"What? A cone of wax? That's ridiculous," someone whispered.

"Two. All exotic forms of dress such as tassels and upturned sandals may no longer be worn."

Kiya gripped my arm. I squeezed her hand tightly in case she felt the need to speak out. Others must have felt the same. There was a buzz of whispers.

Nefertiti sent a razor-sharp glance around the Great Hall to restore quiet before she continued. "It's the custom in Egypt that *adopted* wives from foreign lands retain nothing of their former court."

Kiya shook her head. "It's not about cutting costs. This is aimed at *us*! It's an insult!"

"Three. Silver, lapis lazuli, and emerald may no longer be worn by foreign wives."

Kiya touched her emerald brooch. "But Egypt has no silver or lapis lazuli of its own!" she whispered fiercely. "*We* brought chests of lapis from Mitanni as part of my dowry!"

"Shh! Kiya!"

"Four. Gold worn must be limited to weigh less than a pomegranate. The only person exempt from this rule will be me. It's my duty to wear jewelry suited to a queen."

"And five. Ladies who arrive in court with retinues of serving girls will be required to place some of them into my service." She paused and looked around the Great Hall. "We will now enjoy the dancing." And with that she clapped her hands and ordered the musicians to play and the dancers to begin their performance.

"How can she? No one will steal you from me, Ta-Miu!"

All around me, scarcely hidden by the music of the lyres and harps, a hubbub of angry voices sounded like bees that had had honey stolen from their hive. I watched Wosret as he approached Nefertiti. I could see the dark flush on his face. This was not what he'd planned.

Kiya's eyes flared with anger. "She wants to put us down as if we're nothing but dirt under her feet. She wants to remind us that Egypt overran the kingdom of Mitanni."

"She's playing a game, Kiya. But she's braver than I thought. She managed to anger not just the royal wives but even the highest of high priests as well." I grabbed Kiya's arm. "Quick! They're leaving. We must follow to find out what all this is about."

"You went against my wishes," Wosret hissed as Kiya and I hung back in the portal of the Great Hall.

Nefertiti gave him a sidelong glance. "Wosret, you have such old-fashioned ideas. It's tiresome." She pulled her tunic out of reach of the cheetahs that were clawing at each other around her feet, and swept past him. Then she turned. Her lips lifted at the corners in a playful smile. "*You* don't always behave properly."

He gave her a sharp glance. "What are you referring to?"

Nefertiti raised a perfectly plucked eyebrow and smiled. "I know your secrets."

"Secrets? I have none."

She waved her hand in the air as if batting away a moth, and then laughed. "Did you see the way I commanded the women's attention? How they looked at me? All I did was cast my eye around the room, and everyone fell silent."

Her attendants giggled. Wosret scowled at them. "Keep quiet, you chattering hoopoes. Have you forgotten how to behave in the presence of the highest of high priests? I've matters to discuss with the queen."

The girls quickly bowed.

"My entrance music didn't have enough flourish. Remind me to reprimand the musicians tomorrow."

"Nefertiti, concentrate for a moment." Wosret kicked out at one of the cheetahs. "And send these animals and chattering hoopoes away so we can talk."

"Only if you promise not to lecture!" She clapped her hands and dismissed the attendants with a sweep of her arm. "Off you go. Wait for me in my chambers." She reached up and took the towering vulture crown from her head. "And take this. I can't stand it a moment longer. Its weight has cut a groove into my forehead. I must have another crown. Put my designers on standby."

She nodded curtly at the Nubian slaves. "Keep the cheetahs on cushions at my bedside." Then she linked her arm through Wosret's and fell into step alongside him.

Kiya and I followed in the shadows behind a colonnade.

"Will you listen now?" Wosret demanded.

"I *am* listening, but sometimes you're so *serious*. You behave like an elderly uncle telling me what I can and cannot do. Tonight has been a celebration! My first appearance before all the royal wives. Don't spoil everything by being cross." She grabbed his sleeve. "Look at the lake. It's as if the stars have fallen from the sky. I can see the constellation of the lion and the scorpion in the water."

"The lion and the scorpion are in you, Nefertiti! You have the spirit of the lioness Sekhmet at her fiercest, and at the same time the cunning and ruthlessness of the scorpion goddess, Seqet. You breathe life into the world, but you know just when to sting. Unpredictable. One moment exploding with venom, the next, all charm. You'll make an excellent queen. But you must tame your lion and scorpion spirit. You *must* learn to obey me."

"Stop lecturing, Wosret. Tomorrow we'll show Thebes their new queen. We'll go up and down the Great River on the royal barge." She looked sideways at him and laughed. "With me under the canopy in all my finery, who will resist me?"

5

DAZZLING ATEN

Kiya touched my shoulder. "How do I look? Do you think anyone will recognize me? I'm too afraid to turn my head in case people are staring."

"No one is staring, Kiya. But you shouldn't have come. It's dangerous in the streets of Thebes without protectors."

Kiya curled her lips in protest. "Protectors are for princesses. Today I'm *not* a princess. It's exciting. I'm glad I came. I can judge for myself whether this boy is worthy."

"If we're stopped and questioned, make a run for it before anyone discovers who you *really* are. I'll distract whoever stops us while you escape."

She shook her head. "I won't return to the palace without you."

"You *must*. Thebes is full of brigands on the lookout to make themselves rich. If someone knows you're a princess, they'll capture you and keep you locked up while they bargain for a reward."

She wrinkled her nose. "I'm not at all scared."

"Well, you should be."

The marketplace was busy. Down every side alleyway, people were selling hair trinkets, jars of honeycomb, bowls of cooked lentils flavored with spices. Salt-dried fish and pale delicate blue duck eggs lay in baskets next to platters of ground flour, for those who had no time to grind their own. In the shade of a mimosa tree beneath a sign of the razor, men waited for a turn with the barber.

"Come buy and eat! Taste what's good," a woman urged. She was selling artichokes flavored with dill, lemon, and garlic—and slices of roasted pumpkin as orange and plump as the sun.

"Come if you're thirsty," another woman called out. "Wine and goat's milk. Honey cakes, too, sprinkled with poppy seed."

Kiya took hold of my arm. "Let's taste the honey cakes. They look delicious." She sniffed. "And smell. . . . Someone's baking bread."

"We can't linger, Kiya."

But even at the fish stalls with their stink of rotten fish, she stopped to gawp at the dead silvery fish with their open mouths and entrails spilling out. She stood so close to the flashing knives that she was soon flecked with fish scales.

"Never seen a dead fish before, miss?" A boy scraping a fish goggle-eyed her. "Mind the blood, then. Won't do you no good to get your face all freckled with blood!"

I tugged at her arm. "You'll get proper freckles too. Pull that cloth over your face before anyone recognizes you. You're burning your skin in the hot sun, and now you're covered in fish scales as well!"

She laughed and wrinkled her nose. "Good! I'll

look like a true peasant." Then she nudged me. "Did you see how that boy eyed you?"

"Silly! It was *you* he was looking at, with your glinting halo of fish scales. He fancied you as a fisherman's wife!"

I marched her away from the stalls through a confusing warren of small alleyways, trying to remember where the boy and I had drunk pomegranate juice. What curiosity was driving me to meet him again?

In the morning when I'd told Kiya I was going, she'd sat there in the middle of her large bed with that fierce, stubborn expression I knew so well.

"I'm coming too."

When I'd shaken my head, she'd pouted.

"You're treating me like a child. You're my maid, not my mother. At twelve I'm old enough to make my own decisions. I'm *ordering* you to take me with you."

There was no persuading her otherwise.

We now skirted past some children kicking a ball made of woven reed, with dogs yapping at their heels, and we eventually found the alleyway I was looking for.

The boy was already there, leaning up against a doorway. I was grateful the shadows hid any pink in my cheeks.

"Stop a moment!" Kiya held me back. "I want to see if he meets with my approval." She nodded. "Hmm! Truly handsome. Dark eyes and broad shoulders. I'd have flirted with him too."

"I didn't *flirt* with him. And for the sake of Hathor, don't say too much," I warned her.

He glanced across at Kiya as we approached.

"She's a friend," I said. "A serving girl in the service of Princess Tadukhepa as well. I thought it safer not to come alone."

"If she saves you from donkeys, then you're safer." He bowed toward Kiya. "If this is the beauty of the serving girls, how beautiful must Princess Tadukhepa herself be?"

I noticed Kiya's lips twitch. She held her hand to her mouth when I scowled at her. As he led us through the alleyway down to the river, she made signs behind his back, smiling her approval while I pressed her arm to keep her quiet.

The riverside was busy. Sacks of grain were being off-loaded from boats, and scribes were sitting cross-legged on the ground, calling out numbers as men passed by with heavy sacks on their backs. The river was low, and along the edge, boys were cutting papyrus and trussing and loading the tall plumes into baskets on their backs for the papermakers. With so many plumes sticking up from their shoulders, they looked like papyrus plants themselves.

Women were gutting fish nearby. A herd boy had driven some water buffalo down to the water and was trying to control them as people cursed and shooed them away. A group of women were doing laundry. They rubbed their linen cloths with reed sap and thrashed the cloths against some rocks, sucking at their teeth and puckering their lips as we passed. I felt them taking note of our faces, curious as to why we were idle while everyone else had work to do.

With so many people about, the river was perhaps a bad place for us to go unnoticed.

Kiya turned and stuck her tongue out at the laundry women.

I jerked her arm. "Stop drawing attention."

We stopped in a quiet bend in the river. Brilliant kingfishers flitted about, and some green herons were building a nest. The boy stamped down the reeds and thistles so we could sit comfortably.

I watched the water rushing by and thought of the places it had come from. Perhaps even as far as the rocky cataracts of Nubia, carrying with it smooth black pebbles, desert sand, and drowned water lilies. Perhaps the body of a goat. Perhaps even the body of a man. The same water had touched the stone steps of far-off temples in sunshine and by moonlight and had heard hollow halls echo back its conversation. It had felt the sun's hot kisses and the caress of the wind over its surface, and had tasted the moon's tears.

I thought of Tuthmosis. Perhaps somewhere far in Nubia, he'd drunk from this very same water I was drinking from now.

When I glanced up, I saw the boy watching.

"My name is Samut," he said, as if to break the silence.

A pestilence of flies! I looked at Kiya in dismay. We'd forgotten to choose a name for her.

"Ta—," she began to say, but her voice trailed off as I interrupted.

"Kiya," I blurted out, and shook my head, urging her not to say her proper name—Tadukhepa.

Samut nodded at me. "So you're Kiya." Then he turned to Kiya. "And you're Ta?"

"No!" we both said together.

His eyebrows shot up. "How can you be confused about your names?"

"We're not confused. She's Kiya." I pointed at Kiya. "And I'm Ta-Miu."

"'Little Cat,' of course! So, Ta-Miu, I was nearly right."

I realized the rough peasant tunic had slipped off my shoulder again.

Suddenly Kiya glanced across at Samut with a glint in her eyes. "Are you rich?"

I nudged her. "Hush, Kiya!"

"You must be. Or was the scarab stolen from a mummy wrapping!"

I scowled at her.

She tossed her head. "Or was it given to you by a girl as a token of her heart?"

"Kiya, what's gotten into you?" I said. "Being free of the palace has made you silly."

Samut laughed. "By the white feather of Maat, the answer is no to all three. I'm not rich. Nor a tomb robber. Nor a taker of hearts."

"What *is* your secret, then?" Kiya smiled innocently up at him, wrinkling her nose in the sunlight.

"The scarab was made by a friend who works at

the glass furnaces in the workers' village at the Place of Maat."

I looked up sharply. "The Place of Maat? The village on the west bank? If he lives there, he's an artisan working for the palace. You *mustn't* tell him about us."

Samut's dark eyes glinted like sunlight dancing on the water. Then suddenly he sat up straighter. "Look . . . the royal barge, *Dazzling Aten*, is coming this way."

I scrambled up. Nefertiti! I'd forgotten her plan to appear on the Great River. "Quick, Kiya! This is dangerous! We mustn't be seen!"

"There's no harm." Samut tugged at my arm. "Lie low in the grass. Even if the barge passes as close as that water lily, no one will know you are attendants from the palace. You look like peasant girls. Only I know differently. If Princess Tadukhepa were on board, *she* might recognize you . . . but she's not."

I squinted at Samut. Why did he keep mentioning Princess Tadukhepa? Had he guessed about Kiya?

He shrugged. "If you work for her, she'd know your faces."

Kiya shook her head. She could barely control her bubbles of laughter. "Princess Tadukhepa won't be there. Nefertiti would *never* invite her on the royal barge. She doesn't like her. So there's no harm in watching, is there, Ta-Miu?"

I gave her a sharp look. She'd left us no further option but to stay.

I shielded my eyes from the sun. The boat stood out in dark silhouette against the sunlight, its tall prow curving sharply out of the glittering water like the neck of some strange creature. Two figures stood under the canopy.

Kiya made a spy hole with her fingers. "It's Nefertiti with Amenhotep the Younger alongside her."

The barge slid across the water propelled by about twenty oarsmen. They rowed in a slow measured pace so that the barge seemed to float rather than be rowed. Each time the oars came up, they showered the air with a rainbow of watery jewels.

Crowds had already gathered along the bank, all eager for a view. Everyone pushed for a better place, and children squealed to be lifted up onto their fathers' shoulders, while the old washing ladies grumbled and dug their elbows in until they managed to make a space for themselves in the front.

A ripple of gasps went through the crowd as the

barge drew nearer and every detail of the dazzling designs painted across its sides came into view. The sharp gold upturned prow ended in the shape of an opening lotus flower. The gold canopy had the huge Eye of Horus painted on it. And the vast wings of the vulture goddess, Nekhbet, stretched across the entire red sail, from tip to tip.

Under the protection of each wing were the cartouches of the new king, Amenhotep the Younger, and his queen, Nefertiti.

It was a spectacle not often seen on a workday afternoon. The golden boat made Thebes gleam with its beauty.

Amenhotep was wearing the blue gold-studded Khepresh warrior crown with the gold cobra rising over his forehead. His shoulders had grown broad since I'd last seen him. Across his chest he wore a gold pectoral that flashed in the sunlight.

But it was Nefertiti who commanded the most attention.

Her crown was different from any I'd seen. It rose from her head at a sharp angle, broadening to a flat top, and was decorated with bands of lapis lazuli and carnelian. A gold cobra coiled at her forehead, ready to spit fiery venom into the eyes of her enemies, and another cobra looped down and hung against her cheek. A gossamer-thin tunic left one shoulder entirely bare while the other arm was covered by a sleeve of fine pleats. A broad girdle clasped her tiny waist. On it was the sky goddess, Nut, in blue stones and carnelian against a background of gold.

But it was the crown that made her so different from the old queen. It was the color of the river on a clear day, and even from this distance it drew green from her eyes. Its stark outline worn on her shaved head drew attention to her high cheekbones and long neck.

With eyes out on stalks, the men goggled, and the women seemed to long for a touch of her beauty. The crowd cheered and applauded as the oarsmen dipped their oars and the barge moved forward as stealthily as a crocodile's silent passage.

The queen's image stayed emblazoned on my eye long after the barge had disappeared around a bend in the river. Her heady perfume of lilies and berga-mot and secret blends lingered and drifted on the air.

There was no mistaking her power.

6

THE GODDESS
HATHOR

When I arrived at the temple, old women were sweeping the steps with mimosa branches to ward off the evils of the day. They shook their branches at some boys playing around them. "Be off with you! A plague on your parents for breeding such pests!"

As I passed, one of the women sucked at her teeth and nodded in my direction. "There she is again! That girl! An offering made every day this week to the goddess Hathor. I know a moonstruck girl when I see one!"

One of them leaned on her mimosa branch and cackled out loud. "What do you know about being moonstruck, old Meryt?"

"A frog in your mouth, Senen! I might look as old and worn as these stone steps, but I've done my fair share of making offerings to Hathor, the goddess of love."

"And look what it got you!"

"An old goat of a husband!" she said, and chuckled. "But there were plenty of handsome boys before him."

"By the white feather of Maat, that's true!" one of the women said, and sighed. "But those days are long gone. We should warn the girl that the goddess Hathor is full of tricks. Even fine young men end up as goats!"

As I went up the steps, one of them nodded. "Have you seen who she's after? She meets every afternoon with the boy with the face too handsome for his own good."

My face burned. Couldn't they tell I heard every word they said?

"A lazy boy, if you ask me!"

You were *not* asked, I wanted to snap back, but I bit my tongue.

"He comes from the workers' village at the Place of Maat. But I've never seen him do a day's work. Always hanging around."

"And the girl?"

"Foreign, I'd say! I saw her at the market the same day the Syrian traders came. She has that dark, foreign look."

I stood before the life-size statue of Hathor and blocked my ears. "Hathor, goddess of love, celestial goddess, goddess of women, accept my offering."

I had chosen the figs in my basket with care. Sun-ripened figs were supposed to draw love. Hathor knew about love. I glanced up to see if she was listening. Did I imagine a smile twitching around her mouth?

The women were right. I was moonstruck. Caught in Hathor's web. She had woven a tight net of moon-beams around me.

I had met with Samut every afternoon since the day I'd first seen him.

On my afternoons with him, Samut took me to places I'd never seen before.

We would go to the tomb workers' village at the Place of Maat. A steady *chink, chink* of anvils came from the alleyways leading off behind the houses along the main street. Stonemasons sent up clouds of dust that mixed with the dust from the potters' wheels. And the air was filled with the pungent smell of elm wood shavings from the chariot makers' chisels.

Samut teased and brought words bubbling out of me. Drew them from me.

I told him of the journey from Mitanni. Of the heat and dust. Of how Kiya was wrenched from the arms of her mother. Of how she cried as we were carried in a palanquin on that beastly camel. Down the high mountains and across the plains, along the banks of the Khābūr River with a thousand horsemen. Until we came to the crossing place on the mighty Euphrates River.

"A thousand horsemen!" Samut smiled as if he didn't believe me.

"There *were* a thousand of them," I argued back. "Then we sailed from Tyre in boats across an ocean so wide there was no end to it, and we came to Egypt, where the sea sips up the waters of the Great River. Forty of the three hundred serving girls died along the way from stomach ailments and lack of fresh water. But Kiya's father, Tushratta, cared nothing. All he wanted was the respect of King Amenhotep.

"If you send me gold," he wrote, *"I will give you my daughter. Send me as much as you are able. In your country gold is like dust. You gather it up in armfuls."*

"How do you know he wrote that?"

"I can read. I saw the scroll."

"A girl who reads!" Samut teased.

I smiled back at him. "And then King Amenhotep died during our journey, long before we reached Thebes. And Kiya was passed on to his son Tuthmosis without ever having laid eyes on the king she was sent to in the first place."

"Tuthmosis! Hah! Now he's gone too. Run away. Good riddance, I say."

Samut's outburst surprised me. "Tuthmosis didn't run away. He left because Wosret planned to kill him."

"How do you know?"

"Everyone knows it was the priest from the Temple of Sobek who saved him from Wosret's poison. The priest's daughter, Isikara, went with him. It is Tuthmosis who should be the king, not his brother! Wosret chose Amenhotep because he's young. Wosret knows he can control him. Tuthmosis is the true king."

Samut shook his head.

"It's true. You'll see. Tuthmosis will come back one day and prove it."

"He's too much of a coward."

I bit my lip. Looked away. I couldn't tell Samut how much I knew. About my own part in Tuthmosis's escape.

Samut seemed to guess. He touched the ankh key that hung around my neck next to his glass scarab. "I gave you my heart in the shape of this scarab. Why do you wear that ankh, too? Who gave it to you? Whose heart does the ankh key unlock?"

I didn't dare tell him it was Tuthmosis who had given me the ankh key. I didn't dare tell him how I had helped Tuthmosis escape Thebes. That he had given it to me for protection. In case I needed to hide if it were ever found out I'd helped him.

I shook my head. "The ankh key doesn't unlock a heart."

"What, then?"

"A gate."

"What gate?"

"It's a secret."

He laughed. "You can't keep secrets from me. You'll tell me in your dreams. I will draw your secret like a bee draws essence from a flower."

"Don't be too sure. It's just an amulet. A key shaped like an ankh." I tried to change the subject. "What are those scars and scratches on your arms? Are you a falconer?"

He shook his head. Smiled. "Perhaps I really am a tomb robber. A tomb robber who robs the rich and gives away the jewels and gold to friends."

I laughed back at him. "Stop teasing, Samut. Tombs are well guarded. You'd never get past the guards. And even if you did, you'd never find your way through the labyrinths to the burial chambers. There are too many trapdoors and secret passageways with false doors."

A tomb robber? He was teasing. But all the same I should have been warned in spite of his laughter and denials. But I wasn't. I didn't want to be.

I told Samut of arriving, wretched and miserable, in front of the chief vizier of the Egyptian court. He inspected our gifts of golden chariots and our beasts laden with chests of oils and lapis lazuli. Scribes listed all we had brought and made notes of all we had not brought as well. The list went on and on:

- Twenty chariots with six-spoked wheels
- One hundred trained chariot horses
- Thirty experienced horse handlers
- Forty alabaster jars of myrrh
- One hundred sheep pelts worked to a fine softness
- Three hundred baby lambskins
- One hundred finely woven wool blankets
- Four chests of nuggets of lapis lazuli known as *khesbed*
- One chest of silver bars known as *hedj*
- Ten jars of pine kernel oil
- Five jars of *sef wan* oil extracted from the wood of the Syrian juniper
- Twenty bags of ginger root
- Ten bags of the finest pine resin, for making *kapet* to burn in the temple
- Thirty jars of sweet *bak* oil from Naharin for perfume and cosmetics
- *Nekfitir* oil from Sangar for anointing
- *Gati* oil from Takhsi for anointing

Samut shook his head and smiled as the list got longer and longer.

I told him that when the scribes finally recorded the last gift, we ourselves were inspected. Kiya had her body prodded by various women who clucked at her youthful appearance and pinched her skinny arms.

"No flesh on her!" they complained.

Finally it was Kiya's aunt, Princess Gilukhipa, who rescued us and sent them all away. Gilukhipa had come to the palace of Thebes twenty-six years before and had status beyond many of the others.

I told Samut all this and more. How I wish I'd kept silent.

Finally it was as he said. He drew the secret of the ankh key from me. In truth he *did*.

Not then . . . but later.

7

ANUBIS, JACKAL OF DEATH

A shadow moves through the gardens. The night is moonless. As dark as a river pool.

A sound breaks the silence. The shadow stops. Waits, as silent as a cypress.

Footsteps approach. A guard on patrol. His leather boots make scratching sounds on the gravel of the pathway. Then silence as the guard steps off the pathway and the soft earth takes his footsteps into the night.

The shadow moves forward again . . . avoiding the flares that light every niche and doorway of the palace . . . avoiding the lake, lit up with floating lamps . . . keeping to secret sections of the garden where roses as dark as blood cloud the air with perfume, and in a sudden breeze pale lilies are sails in a sea of darkness.

He knows the route the guard has taken. The shortcut through the courtyard toward the stables. There the guard will meet another guard coming from the opposite direction. If the evening is cold, they will stamp their feet and rub their hands and pull their wool cloaks about them and chat quickly before moving briskly on.

Tonight is warm. Sultry, even. Tonight they will linger. Maybe lean against a pillar and chat about girlfriends or a backstreet brawl where a man was stabbed for looking at another man's wife.

Guards have no fear of men with daggers. They are trained to kill. But tonight killing is far from the mind of the first guard. He has come from the palace kitchen with his stomach full of freshly baked bread the baker's assistant gave him.

The two guards lean up against the pillars. Their voices drift into the night. They don't notice the shadow slipping silently past them.

He must move quickly. Avoid the animal cages. If the monkeys are disturbed and start to howl, they'll bring the dogs running.

He knows the way. Even in darkness his feet are sure of the path.

The stables are ahead. He smells the warm aroma of barley and straw mixed with the smell of horses' breath.

For a moment he pauses. Tempted by the need to run his hands over the flanks of a horse.

Still now he knows the training schedule passed on to him by the Mitannian horse handler. He can recite it. The precise order of rotating trotting with cantering over exact distances with the animal in harness. Done to strengthen the legs and the heart of the horse. The action, long, low, and economical, with very little bend or lift in the knee. The short rest between to relax the horse before another round. And after the training, every horse brushed down and cooled off. Washed in warm water and toweled and fed. He knows the exact proportion of oats to barley and chaff in the morning, midday, and evening feeds.

A stable cat scavenging for mice comes mewing toward him. Rubs against his legs. A horse whinnies.

There is the sound of a door scraping. A stable hand moves about, whistling under his breath, hanging things up, moving brooms, kicking leather buckets into place. The stable hand clears his throat and hawks some phlegm. Then slams the heavy door. The sound of his footfalls disappears into the night.

The shadow stands against a wall for a while, making sure the stable hand won't think of something he has forgotten and turn back.

There are two new horses. He knows they've come from the king of Assyria. Horses as white as freshly washed linen. Whiter than the moon. He wants to see them. It would be safe to enter the stables now. But he can't linger. There are things to get done before the goddess Nut draws the sun into the sky again. He must hurry.

He moves on past the stables.

Even without moonlight he sees the gate ahead. He checks over his shoulder to see that no one has followed. Then he fumbles along the stone wall, feeling for a shelf or niche. He finds what he's looking for. He slips the ankh key into place and hears the click of metal moving against metal. The gate swings stiffly inward into a space as dark as a hyena's mouth.

He fumbles to find the small clay lamp he has carried in his girdle bag. He pushes the gate closed behind and hears the lock click. He waits for his eyes to grow accustomed to the gloom. Then he takes a sharp breath and steps into the darkness as one would plunge into a deep pool. A few paces beyond where the flame can be seen from the entrance, he lights the lamp. He has soaked the wick and put salt in the oil to prevent it from smoking too much.

He holds it high so the glow stretches into the distance. There is no end to the tunnel ahead.

At the entrance to every new passageway, he traces over the stones with his fingers, searching for indents that mark the correct passage.

Three notches, Ta-Miu said.

They are hard to find. Sometimes his fingers mislead him and he needs to retrace his steps.

Suddenly something looms up ahead.

Anubis towers over him. His jackal face dark and his eyes as intense as burning embers. The jackal god carries an ankh in his left hand. The silence is broken by a soft growl, as light as a feather falling, yet it fills the whole chamber with sound.

Follow me. Anubis beckons.

The shadow blinks. Is this truly happening?

There is an altar with a small fire burning. He can smell the scent of cedar. Anubis scatters white powder into the flame. A ball of fire leaps up. Anubis's growls rumble through the chamber like thunder.

I will release your soul so it can fly into the World of the Dead. Swifter than light we will travel with the ferryboat of Ra as it sails to the World of the Dead. Thoth waits there in the Hall of Maat with the Scales of Justice. Time is short. We must be back before morning if you want to live to see the sun of Ra rise over Egypt.

The rock overhead splits open. He feels himself flying upward—a great bird with huge, beating wings, his human head emerging from winged shoulders.

The world is dark and small beneath him. The Great River is nothing but a narrow silver ribbon winding through a landscape of temples smaller than stones. Thebes is a city scraped together by a child's hand. Even the two statues of King Amenhotep guarding either side of his mortuary temple can be scooped up in each hand. Palm trees are as small as the breast feathers of a dove, and cows in fields are no larger than ticks on the back of a dog.

They fly west through the shadowy dip of Abydos.

Below them is the gold boat of Ra glowing with amethyst, emerald, turquoise, and lapis lazuli. The boat is filled with the souls of all who have died that day. He recognizes faces. They are doubles of their earthly faces.

The gates of the World of the Dead are flung wide. Six writhing snakes, each thicker than a man's leg, are curled on either side of the gate, breathing fire and poison. The doorkeeper challenges:

I will not announce thee unless you know my name!

Understander of Hearts is your name! the souls all reply.

To whom must I announce thee? demands the doorkeeper.

To Thoth, the god of wisdom.

As each soul passes through the doorway, Thoth stands with his sharp, curved beak and writes their names on his writing tablet. *Why have you come?* he asks each one.

I am pure of sin, each soul replies.

Thoth leads them to where Osiris sits upon his throne, wrapped in the green mummy clothes of the dead. Osiris wears the spitting cobra on his forehead and holds the scourge and crook across his chest. In front of him are the Scales of Justice. Next to this is Maat, goddess of justice, truth, and order. She wears a white feather on her head. Crouched low on the ground is the terrible monster Ammut, devourer of the dead, with the body of a crocodile and lion and the hindquarters of a hippopotamus.

She waits to snatch hearts that weigh too heavy.

Anubis, the jackal-headed god of death, swoops down toward him.

I'm not dead, he tries to shout. *Remember! You said we must be back before the morning, to see the sun of Ra rise over Egypt. I'm not here to be judged.*

You will be judged if you enter this tomb! Anubis growls. *Say the spells, or Ammut will devour you!*

Ammut bares her teeth. Her snout is bloody.

He tries to remember. He tries to spit out the spells. *I have not disobeyed the gods. I have not stolen from the dead. I have not inflicted pain on anyone. I have not killed.*

Suddenly everything vanishes. There is utter silence.

He has imagined it all. The hideous Ammut has gone. Anubis has gone. All that remains of Anubis is a painting of him on the labyrinth wall.

The heavy weight of the bird wings has dropped from his shoulders. His body is suddenly weak. He blinks hard.

In front of him a sandal is wedged into the crevice of a rock. It holds open a secret door. He pushes the door. It swings open slowly.

A black obsidian statue of Anubis sits with forelegs stretched out in front of him. His jackal ears stand sharply upward. His eyes look straight ahead. His body is as silent as stone.

He guards the well and the secret passage to King Amenhotep's tomb.

8

THE SCALES OF JUSTICE

"Hurry, Kiya! Stop playing with that chameleon. Be quick now. Nefertiti has summoned us."

Kiya sighed as she returned the chameleon to its branch. "The robe you've chosen for me is boring. Can't I wear the cloth you bought at the market?"

I shook my head. "This is not the time for finery. Here, let me look at you. Let's see you haven't broken any of Nefertiti's rules. Don't forget to remove your sandals in her presence. Only Nefertiti, who has no earthly superiors, may wear sandals. We must have our wits about us and pray to Thoth, god of wisdom, that he'll put the right words into our mouths when the time comes to speak."

Kiya pulled at her tunic.

"Stop fidgeting, Kiya."

"I'm anxious."

"There's nothing to be anxious about."

Kiya raised her eyebrow. "But why are we being summoned, Ta-Miu?"

"The messenger didn't say. All he said was that Nefertiti wanted a private audience with you and that I should accompany you."

There were little panicky stars of worry in Kiya's eyes. "What if she's found out you've been crossing the Great River and meeting with Samut?"

"How?"

"A boatman might've guessed your identity and reported you."

I shook my head. "I've bribed the boatmen with figs and pomegranates from my offering basket. I told them I'm a relative of one of the potters from the Place of Maat. Samut explained the potters' methods and the pigments they use for colorants. So if I were questioned, it'd seem as though I've lived all my life in the workers' village and had been brought up in a family of potters."

"Then *why* are we being summoned?"

When we reached Nefertiti's quarters, we were shown to an antechamber outside her receiving rooms.

"Nefertiti is busy with her offering rites," we were told by an attendant.

Through the colonnades we caught a glimpse of her in her private temple, holding her hands up in obeisance and whispering incantations and prayers. Then she strode to her chambers, and we were left with nothing to do but stand and wait for her return.

I saw Kiya bite her lip. I reached out to squeeze her hand. "Don't worry. Making us wait is part of her plan." But I was anxious and nervous too. I'd been reckless in meeting Samut. Now Kiya was involved. Why else *were* we being summoned?

There was a sound of quick footsteps. The door of the anteroom was flung open. Amenhotep the Younger and the highest of high priests, Wosret, came rushing into the room. We swept down to touch our heads to the floor. Attendants brushed the tiles with mimosa branches before them, sprinkled the air with oils, and swung their censers of smoking incense so vigorously I thought I would choke.

Nefertiti emerged in her new towering turquoise crown, accompanied by her fan bearers and the two cheetahs. Amenhotep and Wosret strode forward and led her to her receiving room, with the chief vizier of the palace trailing behind.

We were hurried along after them amidst wafts of incense that had Kiya sneezing all the way.

Nefertiti's lion-footed throne was so impressive that, despite her high crown, she appeared small against its grandeur. She sat too high for her legs to reach the ground, and her feet rested on a plump red-cushioned footstool.

The queen and the highest of high priests conferred in whispers.

Kiya and I looked from one to another in silence. I found myself counting the moments between Kiya's sneezes. As the time grew longer, my mind wandered to the ostrich feather fans, with their long, dark ebony handles held by two small attendants, and to the detail of the throne, with its intricate ivory patterns of flying herons and the high carved back with gold leaf in the shape of a sun, with rays shining down on Nefertiti seated below. I couldn't help smiling when I saw her sandals of delicate gold filigree, adorned with daisies and lotus lilies of lapis lazuli, with tiny ducks and frogs peering out from them.

Suddenly Wosret turned and faced Kiya. His dark eyes flashed. "We have a serious accusation against your maid."

The suddenness of the announcement stopped Kiya's sneezes immediately.

I felt my stomach clench. So this *was* about me!

Kiya pulled herself up as tall as she could before replying. "I'm ready to hear your accusation, my lord."

"Your maid"—he pointed at me—"has been an accomplice to theft of the highest order."

I stepped forward, but Kiya put out a hand to stop me. "Theft?" She shook her head. "Ta-Miu's not a thief! What are you speaking of?"

I held my breath. As a serving girl I was not allowed to speak unless directly addressed. Until I was spoken to I couldn't open my mouth, let alone *question* anything they said.

Kiya shook her head. "Why do you accuse her so unjustly?"

"Unjustly?" His eyes raked across me as if I were a dirty beggar and if his eyes were to rest on me, he'd immediately be contaminated with some awful disease. "It's *she* who has caused injustice. She's stolen from Egypt."

"Stolen? *What* has she stolen?"

"She knows the labyrinth that leads from the palace grounds to King Amenhotep's tomb."

"King Amenhotep's tomb? What has—?"

"Everyone in the palace is aware that she was on friendly terms with Prince Tuthmosis. He knew the labyrinth like the lines on the palm of his hand. As a boy he spent hours playing there when it was being built."

"What has this to do with Ta-Miu?"

"She was planning to run away with him."

I couldn't stop myself. "That's not *true*."

Wosret's eyes bore into me. "Silence! How *dare* you speak!"

Kiya pulled at my tunic and hissed. "Hush, Ta-Miu. I will deal with this."

I shook off her hand. It was odd to have our roles

reversed and Kiya telling me what to do. But all the same I stayed silent.

Wosret nodded at Amenhotep. "Tuthmosis and this serving girl planned it together. They entered the labyrinth after the burial of your father, the king, and stole his treasure."

Amenhotep raised his eyebrows. "That's absurd, Wosret. It makes no sense."

"Allow me to explain. They needed gold and jewels to pay their way so that Tuthmosis could escape."

"*Escape?* But my brother Tuthmosis is *dead*. You led me to believe my brother died of grief at my mother's death."

Wosret waved his hand in the air and hurried on. "Quite so. . . . That's what *I* believed at the time. It's what we *all* believed. It's what we were all *led* to believe by that traitor Henuka."

Amenhotep shook his head. "Henuka wasn't a traitor. He was the priest at the Temple of Sobek. He was present at my mother's embalming."

"How can you know what did or did not happen? You were too young to be there. Henuka told us Tuthmosis had died. But now I know he lied."

"Lied?"

Wosret bowed. "Tuthmosis is alive."

"Impossible!" Amenhotep shook his head. "Why haven't you told me before?"

"We had no proof. I didn't want to upset you. Now the truth is out because of the discovery of this theft. This serving girl helped Tuthmosis steal from his own father's tomb and then helped him to escape up the river to Nubia."

Kiya stepped forward. "By the white feather of Maat, your story doesn't fit with what I know."

"Be silent!" Wosret snapped. "I'm addressing the king."

Amenhotep looked searchingly at Wosret. "It doesn't make sense. Why would my brother steal from my father's tomb, if he was to be king of Egypt himself? He had no need of that wealth."

Wosret shrugged. "I'm sorry to announce your brother's treachery. Your brother didn't want to be king. He was a traitor. I'd have preferred if he were truly dead. I'd have preferred you to think well of him. But you didn't know him as I did. He was devious. He stole because he needed the wealth to build up an army against Egypt."

"An army *against* Egypt? Have you lost your mind?

What proof have you?" Amenhotep asked.

All this time Nefertiti had remained silent. Now suddenly she thrust her hand forward and spoke. "This!"

I gasped. In the cup of her hand was a ring with an emerald so huge, it sparked green against her palm. Samut had given me a similar ring the day before, but it was safely buried under my bed linen. I'd slept with it under my pillow all night, feeling the lump of it, and had hidden it beneath my pallet this morning. It couldn't be the same ring!

"That's my father's ring!" Amenhotep snatched it up from Nefertiti's hand and held it to the light. He glanced quickly at her. "How did you come by it? And what connection is there between my father's ring and this girl from Naharin?"

"She helped Tuthmosis steal it. She kept it after he left."

I clenched Kiya's hand. That's not true! I wanted to shout out. The ring has *nothing* to do with Tuthmosis.

Kiya shook her head. "Impossible! I've never seen this ring before."

Wosret waved his arm in the air as if batting at mosquitoes. "*You* wouldn't have. It belonged to

King Amenhotep. It was buried with him along with all his treasures for the afterlife. But the tomb has been broken into . . . the treasures scattered . . . the best taken. Nothing as large as the golden chariots, of course. . . . Tuthmosis was too devious for that, but the smaller valuables . . . chests of lapis lazuli, the jewel-encrusted daggers, the goblets and gold statues, jewelry . . . have all disappeared. The chief vizier can attest to this. He has a record of everything that was buried with the king. He has drawn up a list of everything that is missing, stolen from right under the gaze of Anubis, jackal of the Underworld, and from under the eyes of the cobra goddess."

Wosret's eyes flashed as he paused and glared around the room. "Who but the son of a king would *dare*? This robbery was planned by Tuthmosis."

Kiya's voice broke the silence. "This has *nothing* to do with Ta-Miu."

I could not believe her bravery.

Wosret's eyes darted toward her. "Your maid was Tuthmosis's friend. She knew his plans. She helped him escape on the day of the Sophet Festival when everyone was at the Temple of Amun. This ring is the proof. This ring was in her possession. There's no other like it."

Kiya shook her head. "I've never seen her with it."

Nefertiti narrowed her eyes and looked directly at Kiya. "Nor would you! You're just a child. What would you know of such things? Your maid is devious! She kept it hidden from you. But one of my ladies saw it on her finger out in the garden last night. She noticed the incredible dazzle of the emerald in the moonlight. No other gem would reflect such sparkle. While we kept you waiting here, we searched your quarters and found it tucked under her bed linen. We need no further proof."

Kiya turned to me. Her eyes begged me to be innocent.

Wosret nodded. "She's guilty of tomb robbery. She has defiled the king's tomb. If King Amenhotep is not properly received into the afterlife, it'll be *her* doing. She has defiled the sanctity of his tomb."

"*No!*" I couldn't stop myself.

"Be silent!"

Kiya tugged hurriedly at my tunic and managed to keep her voice calm. "You're mistaken, my queen. The ring must have been placed there by someone else. If Ta-Miu were guilty of tomb robbery, I'd know. I know all her secrets. She has been at my side since we were children."

Nefertiti surveyed Kiya coldly. One eyebrow lifted high into the dark curve of a kestrel's wing. "If that is so, then you would know where she's been going when she leaves the palace every afternoon."

I heard Kiya's sharp intake of breath. "How can you possibly know?"

"So you *do* admit she leaves the palace? We were suspicious and put a guard on her, but she's managed to lose him each time."

"This has *nothing* to do with the ring, my lord." Kiya turned to Amenhotep. "Allow my maid to speak for herself."

Amenhotep nodded. "Let's hear her, then."

Wosret held the ring beneath my face. "Have you seen this ring before?"

I swallowed hard. How could I explain without telling them it was Samut who had given it to me? I nodded. "I have."

Kiya's eyebrows shot up. She clutched my arm. "You couldn't possibly have, Ta-Miu. What are you saying? Please tell me it was placed under your pallet by someone else."

Nefertiti regarded us coolly. "Clearly your maid is not as innocent as you believe. Not only has she seen it, but she's also worn it."

I shook my head. "I . . . I can't deny this. But—"

Kiya gripped my hand. "Ta-Miu, I beg you. You're *mistaken*."

I couldn't meet Kiya's eyes. I looked down at the floor pattern of herons and lotus lilies. It was a scene of peace far removed from this turmoil. "I'd like to say I'm mistaken . . . but I'm *not*." The words came out hot on my breath.

Wosret's eyes flashed triumphantly. "So you stole it from the labyrinth?"

I shook my head.

"Then, how do you come to possess it?"

I thought of what I'd said to Samut when he'd first held it out. *I can't possibly accept this. Not one so large! The jewel is the size of a pigeon's egg.*

A girl as beautiful as you deserves nothing better, he'd answered.

We'd been sitting in the shade of a pomegranate tree. Even in the shade the jewel had sparked and sent flashes of green fire against my skin.

Samut had closed my fingers over the ring. *It's the fire burning in my heart. Keep it hidden. Look at it to remind you of me.*

I had hidden the ring in my girdle bag all the way home. Then, last night, as I'd walked in the gardens, I'd taken it out secretly and placed it on my thumb—the only finger it fitted. The moonlight had sent sparks of green fire through it.

Now Wosret was asking again. But I *couldn't* say Samut had given it to me. How could I admit I'd told him about the labyrinth gate? That my ankh key was a duplicate of a key kept just inside the gate?

I couldn't accuse him. I didn't know for sure. Would Samut have *dared* to enter the tomb? I had to ask him first. He'd have a reason for how he had gotten the ring.

He wasn't a tomb robber. He'd been joking when he'd said he was. Surely someone had given it to him. A jeweler friend? Maybe the ring was a copy.

"Answer me!" Wosret demanded.

I shook my head. "I . . . I . . . can't say!"

Wosret put his face close to mine, so close I smelled the garlic on his breath. "You *can't?* You mean you *will* not!"

"I'm sure it's a copy. It *can't* be the real ring."

"How would a maid know the difference between a copy and the real ring? And besides, how did you get possession of a copy?"

"It was given to me by a friend of a jeweler."

Nefertiti raised an eyebrow. "If it's a copy, why is the real ring missing from the tomb?"

Wosret nodded. "There's only one answer. Tuthmosis stole it with the rest of the treasure that's missing from his father's tomb. This girl knew of the tomb robbery. To keep her quiet Tuthmosis gave her the ring as his parting gift when he escaped."

Wosret's lizard eyes darted triumphantly over me. He turned to Amenhotep. "I was right to appoint you as king in your brother's place. Tuthmosis is nothing but a tomb robber. And this girl is no better."

Amenhotep raised his hand. "Wosret, until we have complete proof, I ask you *not* to accuse my brother of theft."

Wosret bowed. "You are young and have been protected from the evils beyond the palace walls. Let me handle this. This girl must be imprisoned for life for such treachery against the kingdom of Egypt."

"No!" Kiya's voice sounded strangled. "Please, my lord, I beg you!" She fell at Amenhotep's feet.

Wosret cut across her words. "Get up at once. You have no say in this!"

Amenhotep touched Kiya's shoulder. "Let Princess Tadukhepa speak. As a royal wife she is entitled!"

"Entitled?" Nefertiti stood up so briskly that the amethysts swinging from her ears flared as they caught the light. Her eyes matched their flare. "Entitled by what? No, Amenhotep! Listen to me, your first royal wife. She can't be trusted. She tried to protect her maid and denies what we've discovered. It's unforgivable. We don't have to listen to her. Tadukhepa's a child! A foreign child, at that! And a liar."

"Nefertiti, stop. We must be as fair and wise as Thoth weighing the Scales of Justice. It's our duty to hear all sides before we come to a conclusion. Princess Tadukhepa's maid will be held in prison until we know the *exact* truth. If she's innocent, she'll be set free."

My heart turned to stone. I was to be held captive . . . until I was proved innocent. But who could prove me innocent? Only Samut.

9

THE PRISON

Samut has charm. His charm led me astray. Now I was in prison. Not even Kiya's speaking up could save me from Nefertiti's decision.

"Charm" is a strange word. A charm can be a trinket to ward off evil. Or it can be a spell that protects or brings evil to the person it's used against.

But it's also something that has the power to delight and fascinate.

Samut had given me a charm for protection, but he had also charmed and fascinated me.

Kiya had told me right away to perform the sacred ritual to bring out the magic of the scarab Samut had given me.

I had covered an olive wood table with a pure linen cloth and put censers of myrrh in the middle of the table, as well as a jar of chrysolite, into which I'd mixed an ointment of lilies and cinnamon. I had taken the amulet and laid it in the ointment. Had left it for three days. Then I had removed it and anointed myself with the mixture early in the morning and recited the prayer of the scarab. Afterward I had made a sacrifice of fresh bread and seasonal fruits threaded on vine sticks.

I had done all this.

But it had been false. Despite the ritual, the scarab *hadn't* protected me.

"Scratch, scratch, scratch! That's all you do. Are you listening to me? I'm your neighbor. Here in the cell next door. What are you doing?"

The voice was insistent, but I didn't want to speak.

"No amount of scratching on the walls will get you out. What are you doing?"

"Writing."

"What?"

"Words."

"Are you a scribe? Are you making lists?"

"No."

"What do you write, if not lists?"

"Words to help me understand."

"Understanding doesn't come from *words*. Understanding is in the *head*. So you might as well stop your writing now."

I threw down the ankh key. It was just my luck to have a talkative neighbor!

I paced out the steps. The cell was exactly six paces by five, and by the looks of the scum lines on the thick mud brick walls, it had once been flooded.

"*Now* what are you doing?"

"Walking."

There was the sound of a dry laugh. "Walking won't get you out. They've done it before, you know. Backward and forward. Pacing is useless. No amount of pacing has ever gotten anyone out. Just wears out your sandals."

I scratched at the paving stones with my bare hands. Every tile was fixed. And the walls were solid.

The only light came in through a narrow slit at ceiling height. Too narrow for even the smallest shoulders to squeeze through. I pulled the bed pallet across and rolled it up to give extra height.

"*Now* what is it that you're doing?"

"Looking out."

"Hah! I know. You're standing on the bed pallet. I've done that too. But I've given up. All you see are feet passing by. Ugly, they are."

"What?"

"The feet. Never see any pretty feet. It's all calluses and veins and filthy uncut toenails that pass by here. Feet with mud between the toes looking as if they've walked through a cow barn. This is a poor part of town. You won't see jeweled toes or ankle bracelets in these parts."

I stood on tiptoe and had a glimpse of glinting water between clumps of reed and papyrus. The prow of a boat slipped past. A distant *shrr, shrr* sound of sistrums and chanting voices told me I was near one of the temples.

"Do you hear them? It never stops. Could drive an old woman mad. But I'm used to it."

The cell was hot and stank of urine and more

besides, and there were flies everywhere. I shooed as many as I could out the narrow slit opening and tore a strip off my tunic and tied it over the bars to prevent more from entering.

"What do you look like? Even if I squeeze my head against my cell gate, I can't catch a glimpse of you. Your voice sounds young."

I sighed as I picked up the ankh again. "I *am* young."

"Are you writing again?"

I ignored her. It was more than just sistrums and chanting that could drive a person mad. She was making my thoughts churn with her chattering.

I threw down the ankh again and flung myself down onto the straw pallet, but jumped up soon enough. It felt as if my body had been rubbed with burning chilies. I was itching all over and covered in red bumps. It came from more than just palm fibers that stuck through the woven covering of the pallet.

"Hah! I can hear they've got you! You'll get used to them. Eventually you don't even bother to scratch. Just let them crawl and bite."

How long would I have to endure this? The only

washing facility was a stone trough of dirty water and a gutter that sloped toward a stinking hole in the floor. Even the lowliest of servants in the palace had better toilet facilities.

It was no good shouting or shaking the gate. I had tried both, but the guards, who sat just out of sight, had ignored me.

"No good putting up a fuss, deary," the woman had called out. "They'll take no notice of you. Doesn't do any good to show you're feisty. Save your breath. Just shut your mouth and take what you get."

"It's *unjust*! I haven't committed any crime! I can prove it."

"That's what they *all* say. Those down the corridor don't care whether you're guilty or not! I should know. Been here long enough now!"

"How long?" I jabbed the ankh at the mud brick.

"Can't say exactly. I can't write, but I scratch marks on the walls, take note of the festivals. I think I've seen seven Sophet Festivals go by."

"Seven! You've been in this place for *seven* years?"

"Maybe more, deary! Who knows?"

"What did you do to be put in prison for so long?"

"Stole some bread."

"Bread? You've been here for *seven* years for stealing bread!"

"I think they've forgotten me. I've no family to plead my cause."

"Praise Horus! Don't let them forget me, too! Samut will come for me."

"Ah, Samut! And would that be your young man? Don't depend on it. Young men find new girlfriends that cause less trouble."

I leaned my forehead against the cool mud bricks. I hadn't caused trouble. I wasn't to blame. I *had* to speak to Samut. My last words to Kiya had been "Tell Samut they've taken me."

"Not speaking now. Sulking, are you? Why are you here, then?"

I wouldn't answer.

"Sulk, then! I'll use my imagination. Let's see . . . Was it for—"

"They say I stole a ring from King Amenhotep's tomb," I snapped before she could reel off a list of possible offences.

"Stole King Amenhotep's ring! From his tomb! Good Horus deliver you! All I did was steal a loaf of bread. *Tomb robbing!* You'll be here for more than seven years, deary!"

"I'm *not* a tomb robber!"

"But you took it."

"But I *didn't!* The ring was given to me."

"Hah! By a tomb robber, no doubt!"

"Samut's no tomb robber!"

"Ah, the boy again! Now you're protecting him. Well, he won't come for you. Believe an old woman's word. He'll be protecting his own skin. You won't see the likes of him here."

"That's not true. He has to come." I shook the gate. I would've shaken her too if I'd been able to lay my hands on her.

"That's what they all say! No, you'll have to think of someone else to save you! That's what boys are like. They leave you when the luck turns bad."

I turned away from the gate.

"Now you've gone silent again. Is it something I said to upset you? It's the truth, though. Don't stop talking. It's been lonely here. The girl who was there before you was a very silent creature. Then she died."

I held my hands to my ears and flung myself back

onto the pallet. She was wrong! Samut *would* come! Kiya would make sure. They wouldn't let me stay here for seven *hours* . . . let alone seven *days* . . . or . . . Hathor help me . . . seven *years!*

"Oh, well. When you feel like talking, I'll be here. Not going anywhere myself. My old bones will rot before *I* get out!"

I beat my fists into the pallet and stifled my sobs against the filthy fabric. *Sekhmet, fighting lion spirit of Hathor, save me. Seventeenth lion, save me! Claw at my enemies! Bring Samut to me riding on your back!*

I slipped down onto the floor and lay my hot cheek against the stone. High above me I watched a pair of muddy woven sandals walk past and heard the *clip-clop* of donkey hooves. Flies buzzed around my face. Voices of the temple priestesses intoned endlessly, and words hammered in my head. *Samut will come! Samut will come! He will!*

I was tired. I needed sleep. Tomorrow I would think straight again.

Jealousy is something that eats at you. It makes you protective, afraid, suspicious, and intolerant. And at all times vigilant.

Nefertiti could not get rid of Kiya, but she had rid herself of me. She'd scored a victory over Kiya. I should have known better. Yet I'd trusted Samut. How would I get out of prison and prove my innocence without revealing his guilt?

"There you go! You've started up again. I can hear you. Scratch. Scratch. Scratch. Leave it be. Just mark up the days and leave it be. That boy's not coming. Believe me. Take an old woman's advice. How many days has it been now? You might as well get used to being here. He's not going to come."

A pestilence of flies on this woman! What did she want from me?

I looked at the few words I'd carved into the hard-baked mud brick wall. The strokes were uneven. The point of the ankh didn't make a good stylus. But if I died here, it would be a record. The ramblings of a servant who'd once lived at the palace. A girl from Mitanni. A girl who'd trusted a boy. A boy with great charm.

I hadn't carved the letters of his name. That way no one would know. He wouldn't be blamed.

Isis kept her brother alive by remembering him. If I could just keep Samut alive, he *would* come.

If he didn't? Words wouldn't help keep *me* alive. By the time someone read the words, I'd long be dead.

"You're very silent this morning. Are you keeping your strength up? It doesn't help to get weak. The bread they bring us is stale and the goat meat stringy. But you need to eat. I knew a girl . . ."

Keep quiet, old woman, I wanted to shout. Instead I clenched my teeth and clutched my fingers around the ankh and began gouging more words into the hard-baked wall. My hands were rough and cracked. There was dirt under my nails.

It was pointless. I jabbed the ankh into the wall.

Why won't he come? Where is he? Why has he left me here to rot?

"Are you crying? Doesn't help to cry, deary."

PART TWO

PART TWO

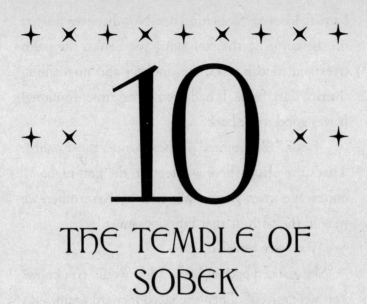

10

THE TEMPLE OF SOBEK

Isikara sat up front in the reed boat with Tuthmosis behind her. The wind in her face carried a perfume of lotus lilies, reeds, and damp earth. It had blown stiffly every day since they'd left Nubia. But the current had been strong enough to drive them downstream without the need for strenuous paddling.

She felt a stirring of excitement like butterfly wings brushing against her throat. Nubia and the battlefields were far behind her. Now her eyes feasted on the color of the soil along the banks, the palm trees and mud houses, the donkeys and men tilling the rich dark fields. It had been a long time. Too long! It was good to be back.

"Look." She pointed. "There! Under those palms. That's the place where we slept on the first night of our escape when Wosret was after us. Remember, we were in the path of that hippopotamus."

"You were terrified."

She glanced back at him. "How would you know? You were asleep!" Then she faced forward again. "It's strange to be back. Do you think anyone will recognize us?"

"You don't look like the girl who left with me."

"What did she look like?"

"She was fair-skinned. Pretty."

"And?" She hit down hard with her paddle to splash Tuthmosis, and the boat nearly tipped. "What am I now?"

"You're as sunburned as a peasant girl who's worked in the fields all her life. Just as well. No one must recognize us. Until I've spoken secretly to my brother, no one must know we've returned. If

Wosret gets a hint of us being in Thebes, I won't live long enough to draw a breath, let alone speak to my brother."

"What will you tell Amenhotep?"

"The truth. That Wosret tried to poison me. That Wosret wanted him as king in my place because he was young enough to control."

"Amenhotep will think you've come to take the throne from him."

Tuthmosis shook his head. "My brother's not a fool. He knows my father was suspicious of the Priests of Amun. But my father was powerful enough and the priests were scared enough of him not to step out of line. He believed Thebes should honor a single god."

"Amun-Ra, the sun god?" Isikara shrugged. "We *all* believe in the sun god."

Tuthmosis shook his head. "Not Amun-Ra but Aten, the sun itself. Remember, my father named his royal barge *Dazzling Aten*."

Isikara almost dropped her paddle. She twisted around to stare at him. "No one can honor the sun directly. The priests would *never* allow it."

"Exactly! That's why I must meet my brother. If

Aten is the single god of Thebes, there'll be no need for the Priests of Amun. He can get rid of them."

"*What?* What about the three gods Amun, Mut, and Khonsu?"

"They'll no longer be important."

Isikara sucked in her breath. "The three gods of Thebes? No longer important? Are you serious? Wosret will *never* stand for it. Tuthmosis, you *can't* speak out. They'll kill you."

"I'm in danger whatever happens. Wosret tried to murder me. The priests have been plotting for a long while to control Thebes. I must protect the throne of Egypt. I *have* to meet my brother before Wosret discovers we've returned. Now, keep paddling, Isikara, or we'll never reach the Place of Maat before nightfall."

"The Place of Maat? I thought we were going to the palace so Ta-Miu could help us."

"It's too risky. It's better to stay in the workers' village. I know some artisans there who worked in my father's tomb. They'll protect us. I can trust them."

She turned to look back at him. "I've a favor to ask. Can we do one thing first?"

"What?"

"Can we stop at the Temple of Sobek?" Before he could interrupt, she went on. "Please, Tuthmosis. It's just around this bend in the river. I need to. Perhaps all the rumors we heard in Nubia were untrue. Maybe my father's still alive. Maybe he's there."

"You can't truly believe this?"

Isikara shrugged.

Tuthmosis shook his head. "It's too dangerous. We can't stop. What if we're spotted?"

"I *must*. Even if it's just to ask for the blessing of the crocodile god, Sobek."

"We don't need the blessing of Sobek."

She turned her back on him and began paddling again.

Tuthmosis slapped his paddle against the water. "You're so stubborn! Have your way, then. But let's be quick."

When the tall, familiar columns of the temple appeared ahead, with the river lapping its wide stone steps, Isikara and Tuthmosis lifted their paddles and allowed the boat to drift forward in silence toward the wooden quay.

The walls of the sacred crocodile pool alongside the bank had been neglected. There were gaps, and stones missing. Any crocodiles taken for ritual washing would have easily escaped into the river.

Isikara clutched at her amulets and said a quick silent prayer. *Great Sobek, forgive me. I left your temple because I had to escape Thebes. It's not my fault you've not been properly served.*

"It looks as if no one has made offerings to Sobek for a long while. We must be careful," she whispered. "Sobek's a fierce god. He could take revenge." She searched around the boat for bubbles coming to the surface. It was a sure sign a crocodile was lurking under the water. "Keep watch while I swing the boat toward the quay. Search the banks, too. We don't want to meet a crocodile unexpectedly. Remember how my brother lost his arm."

"We're *not* stopping, Isikara. Pray quickly for a blessing from the boat and let's move on."

"I *can't* just pass by. Perhaps my father's there."

"The place is a mess. You can see he's not. It's too dangerous. Wosret could have spies looking out for us."

"It'll be more dangerous if we *don't* stop. We *have* to show Sobek respect."

"You can see the temple's not being used. No one is worrying about Sobek any longer."

"Tuthmosis, trust me! We *have* to honor Sobek! I know it in my bones!" Isikara grabbed at some reeds and drew the boat to the quay.

At the same time Tuthmosis wedged his paddle against the quay to try to hold the boat back from it. But she took a huge leap and landed on the wooden boards. "I'll be fine."

"Don't be foolish, Isikara! You don't know for sure!"

She tossed her head and stared back at him. His crystal blue eyes took on an opaque, smoky color. She knew that look. "Stay in the boat, then. I'll go alone!" She turned and hurried along the rough planks. They were beginning to split and crack. At the stone steps she glanced back over her shoulder. "I won't be long."

It was useless trying to stop her. He watched as she passed into the dark shadow of the temple.

A breeze shivered through the reeds, rustling the papyrus heads back and forth. A few green-backed herons were nesting between the reeds, and there were circles in the water as fish surfaced to gulp at flying insects. Two pied kingfishers hovered above, then plummeted down to dive at the fish.

Tuthmosis checked the height of the sun above the palm trees on the western bank. It was sinking fast. It would be dark by the time they reached Thebes. This was a waste of time. Wosret would already know his army had been defeated in Nubia. He would also know he and Isikara were still free. What if this were a trap? Wosret might've guessed Isikara would stop at the temple.

He tied the boat firmly against a post and strode up the stone steps after her.

The temple was shadowy and smelled of wet earth and dampness. He paused so his eyes could get used to the gloom. Bright shafts of sunlight fell across the floor. They made the dark corners seem even darker.

"Isikara!" he whispered urgently.

The river had clearly risen higher than the steps recently and flooded in. Black mud and debris lay scattered across the stone floor. There was no knowing what was in the other chambers . . . who might be lying in wait.

A breeze rustled some dry strands of reed at his feet. A bread offering and some shriveled lotus flowers lay strewn across an altar. A life-size carving of the crocodile-headed Sobek stood upright. He wore a headdress with a horned sun disk. Tuthmosis felt the god's eyes follow him as he crossed the court-yard.

"*Isikara?*" he whispered into a dark chamber. His voice echoed back hollowly. There was no sound of footsteps, but the floor had drag marks in the dirt. He peered down a stone stairwell. A few broken pottery jars lay discarded below. An imprint of a foot had dried hard in the layer of mud on the steps. Beyond that were shapes that seemed to be small mummified crocodiles wrapped in linen strips. They were lined up on shelves around the walls, like loaves ready to be baked.

A sudden hiss of breath behind him made him spin around.

He was standing face-to-face with the largest crocodile he had ever seen.

It lay wedged along a narrow stone shelf, its head raised in strike posture, with its mouth open and its teeth exposed in a wide evil grin. It fixed him with eyes that glowed red in the half gloom. He could smell the fetid, rotting meat stench of its breath.

He glanced quickly to where he'd entered. The passage wasn't wide enough for him to get safely past again. This was it. He would never live to tell his brother the truth. There was no escape.

Another hiss came from the crocodile's mouth. Tuthmosis heard the click of the jaws opening wider.

Then, lightning-fast, it lunged. But just as its head came forward, it seemed to choke in midair. From the corner of his eye, Tuthmosis caught a glimpse of Isikara. She had thrust a branch at the crocodile's throat. A fork in the branch pinned its head against the stone wall. Its jaws were clamped shut. Its legs slithered to get a grip on the slimy stone shelf.

"Get around him! Quick!" Isikara spat. "I won't be able to hold on much longer."

Tuthmosis felt as if his legs had turned to stone. Then suddenly he was there beside her. He tried to grab the branch from her.

"Get away!" she shouted. "If I lose my grip now, he'll get both of us. As long as I can keep his jaws clamped, he's under control. Run!"

"Kara, please . . ."

The crocodile was thrashing its huge tail. But the narrow space and the wet slippery stone was hampering it.

"Get a rock!" she shouted. "I have to wedge the branch so we delay him. Hurry! I can't hold much longer!"

A rock? He looked around. Then heaved a stone off the broken wall and rolled it across the paving. For a moment it seemed too late. Isikara was losing her grip. But then the rock was up against the wall and the branch wedged tightly behind it. And without stopping to check whether it held, they sprinted out through the temple and down the steps to the boat.

Tuthmosis fumbled as he tried to loosen the rope that held the boat. Then suddenly they swung free out into the river away from the quay.

When he looked back, the crocodile was already slithering down the steps after them. At the quay it lifted its heavy body high on its legs and ran along the bank in a strange doglike way before plunging into the water. But they were far out in the main stream now, where the current was swifter. No matter how fast it swam, it wouldn't catch them.

They dug their paddles hard into the water. Tuthmosis heard Isikara breathing hard. His own breath was still coming in short, jerky gasps. Eventually he found his voice. "How did you know what to do?"

"I went looking for the forked branch my brother

and I used to control the crocodiles in the pit . . . just in case I needed it." Then she laughed. "So it was luck that I found it. Perhaps my prayers to Sobek were answered after all."

Ahead of her on the western bank the sun was a ball of fire skimming just above the horizon. On the eastern bank a full moon rose, huge, and as red as a split pomegranate, like a second sun in the sky. The sun and moon hung low on the horizon on either side of the wide river . . . glowing as red as crocodile's eyes in the dusky light.

The Eye of the Sun and the Eye of the Moon. The two wedjat Eyes of Horus.

The eyes seemed a warning of what was still to come. What lay ahead of them in Thebes?

11

THE PLACE OF
MAAT

It was late by the time they arrived at the quayside on the western bank of Thebes. The men who hired out donkeys had gone home for the night.

The moon was already high and small in the sky as they walked the long dusty road toward the Place of Maat. Even the stars seemed remote.

Isikara cursed herself for being so headstrong. If she hadn't been so insistent on stopping at the

Temple of Sobek, they would have been safely asleep in the village by now, instead of dragging their feet through the dust in the middle of the night.

Tuthmosis seemed to sense her agitation. He turned and smiled. "It's all for the best that we're so late. Everyone is asleep. No one will see us."

In the moonlight she caught sight of a silvery jackal crossing the roadway ahead of them. It stopped for a brief second to stare at them, and then went hurriedly on. Just as suddenly she saw small lights bobbing where the road took a bend around some boulders.

Tuthmosis pulled her down. "Quick! Hide against the boulders. They're coming this way."

Her heart beat high in her throat. "Who?"

Tuthmosis shrugged. "Soldiers, perhaps."

She saw him finger the hilt of the dagger hidden beneath the folds of his tunic.

"Soldiers? Out in the middle of the night?"

"On patrol, perhaps."

"Looking for us? How would anyone know we've returned?"

"Wosret has spies. They could've seen us on the river."

Isikara grabbed hold of his arm. Only a few boulders lay between them and the path along which the men were coming. It *had* to be a search party. Why else were the people carrying lamps, and why were there so many of them?

And now Isikara caught sight of the coppery glint of weapons, slung across the men's shoulders and hanging from their girdles. And as the men drew closer, she felt the heavy tramp of their feet on the earth beneath her sandals.

"What'll we do?" she growled.

"Take this dagger. I have another."

Her stomach twisted. A dagger? She hadn't used a dagger since that night in the desert in the Medjay camp. Even now the thought of the dark blood, seeping through the man's tunic and staining her hands, turned her to stone.

No! She couldn't use a dagger again. Not ever. Not even to defend her life!

"Take it!" Tuthmosis spat. "You *have* to, Isikara."

"I *can't!*" She could hear the hoarseness in her voice. "I *can't* do this, Tuthmosis! Not again!"

She felt his hand grip her arm. "You must!"

As he spoke, the group of men drew level with

the boulders. Suddenly they veered away on another path she hadn't noticed.

She felt her body go slack and all the breath leave her.

In the moonlight Tuthmosis was grinning and shaking his head. "They weren't soldiers. Did you see? They were workers, carrying implements and chisels for hacking rock. They're stonecutters."

"Stonecutters?"

He nodded. "Going to work in the royal tombs."

"At this time of night?"

"The tombs are dark. What does it matter whether it's day or night when you work by lamplight deep inside a mountain? They work shifts all through the night."

He led her back onto the deserted road where moments ago the men had tramped. Then they passed the village well and went through the north gate. The village was silent and lit only here and there by lamps. Dark, narrow alleyways led away from the single main road.

Tuthmosis seemed sure of his way. He came to a mud brick house and tapped lightly on the door. There was a rough mud-sculpted cobra above the lintel. A dog started to growl. Tuthmosis picked up a clod of earth and threw it at him. Then a muffled voice called out, "Yes? Who is it?"

"Tut."

Tut? Isikara glanced quickly at Tuthmosis's face. Is this what his friends called him?

The door opened a crack, and a huge tousled-looking young man peered out. He clutched a weapon close to his body. "What? It can't be!"

"It's truly me, Hera. Quick, let us in!"

The door swung back. "Tut! By Horus, I hardly recognized you in your peasant tunic. Where have you come from?" He enfolded Tuthmosis in a lion hug. "What are you doing here? I heard you were lost somewhere in Nubia. And who"—his eyes swept to Isikara—"is this?"

"She's a friend."

"*She?*" He gave Isikara another swift glance. "I thought her a *boy!*"

"Shh! Don't speak so loudly. Your neighbors will hear. Isikara's in disguise too. She's the daughter of the embalmer, Henuka. Quick! Shut the door! We need to be hidden. Just for a few days until I get a message through to my brother."

Hera turned and fumbled with a lamp until it was finally lit and the small room took on a glow. "I thought you were at war in Nubia, but here you are! Have you come to claim your throne back from Amenhotep?"

Tuthmosis shook his head.

Hera raised an eyebrow. "If not to claim the throne, what, then?"

"I must warn Amenhotep of Wosret."

"You must clear your name of scandal too. There are all sorts of rumors. They say you took up arms against Egypt."

Tuthmosis nodded. "That's true."

"What?"

"There's a lot to explain. But first I need to confront Wosret and get him to admit he tried to poison me. That he planned my death so my brother could be king."

Hera shook his head. "Hah! You might as well ask a statue to come to life. Wosret will *never* admit it. He has too much to lose. He needed a young king he could tame. He seems to be taming Nefertiti as well."

"All the more reason to meet with Amenhotep quickly. Will you hide us?"

Hera gave Isikara a quick look. "*Both* of you? This is a household of workmen. I've seven brothers. We'll be too rough for her."

Isikara tossed her head. "I'm used to men. I fought in the Nubian army. Besides, I've a brother. I'll cope."

"You'd be better off with a woman. There's not much space here. It's easier to hide one person rather than two. When we go off to work or sleep in shifts, the village is full of wives and children. I've an aunt you can stay with. She travels to Thebes often. She works there as a temple chantress. You'll be safe with her."

Isikara looked across at Tuthmosis. "I . . ."

"Hera's right. It'll be safer if we split up."

"But . . ."

"It's only until I speak to my brother. Once he's on our side, we won't have to hide."

"But we've been together since . . ." Her voice faltered. She felt the warmth rising in her cheeks.

Hera laughed as he looked between them. He gave Tuthmosis a shove. "Have you fallen in love? Come! Let's make plans before the dawn shift of workmen wakes up. There's a new fellow to look out for. He's the new vizier here at the Place of Maat. A fierce fellow by the name of Ramose."

"What happened to the last vizier?"

"Wosret got rid of him. Said he was soft and taking bribes. It suited Wosret to put a friend in his place. The new vizier sits as magistrate of the local court. He has appointed a whole phalanx of foremen. Guards responsible for overseeing the removal of tools from the royal storehouse, and scribes who distribute our food wages and who take note of anyone dodging work. There are always squabbles about deliveries of fish and beer and grain and wood for fuel. But play your game right and you get extra luxuries of salt and sesame oil. But still . . . I warn you the new vizier is a tough one to handle. He has spies everywhere."

Tuthmosis nodded. "We'll be sharp and pray to the cobra goddess who lives at the top of your mountain to protect us."

THE PRISON—KIYA

re you there? Wake up now. You've been sleeping all morning. I heard someone asking for you. Listen now. Is that your boyfriend's voice? He's demanding to see you."

It wasn't Samut's. It was Kiya's voice. I felt a flare of hope.

Yet when I looked up, it wasn't Kiya standing in front of me at the gate, but some urchin boy with a short rough wig and a ragged, coarse tunic that covered his chest, and a girdle and leather bag about his waist. His face was smeared with dirt.

"What do you want with me?" I snarled, and sank back onto the stone floor.

"Ta-Miu? It's me."

"Kiya?" I looked up again. "Is that truly you?"

"Shh! Don't say my name so loudly. So my disguise fooled you, too." She grinned back and reached through the bars. "You look awful. Don't they feed you? Don't you wash?"

I gripped the gate. "Get me out of here!"

"And your hands are bleeding. What have you done to them?"

"Her hands bleed because she scratches at the wall. Words, she says. All day long more words. Scratch, scratch, scratch. And doesn't eat. Not that I mind. The guards give her food to me. Can't let it go to waste! Pig's swill, that's what it is. But a person has to eat. Come here! Let me look at you. You're not Samut, are you? No, I don't imagine you are. Too young to be Samut. Cheeks too smooth. Hands too dainty and voice not yet broken in. Stand closer so I can see you. You wouldn't be a girl, would you?"

"I'll keep my distance, thank you. And no, I'm not a girl. I'm a *boy!*"

I shook my head at Kiya "Take no notice of the old woman. She's been here seven years. She listens to everything I do. I can't move without her saying something."

Kiya turned to the woman. "I'll ask you not to listen while I speak to my sister. If I share some of the food I brought, will you keep away and busy yourself in the back of your cell?"

"Your *sister?* Hmm. She said nothing of a brother. Why haven't you come before now?"

"I don't have to explain to you. And I *am* her brother!"

"A cheeky boy, at that! Give me the food, then. If it's worth it, I won't listen in. I'll stay away."

"Give it to her, Kiya. She can have my share. I'm not hungry."

"No. You must eat, Ta-Miu. I've brought smoked duck and peacock hearts, and honey cakes and grapes for their sweetness."

"*What?* Did I hear properly?"

"I asked you not to eavesdrop."

"But smoked duck and peacock hearts! By the

feather of Maat, can it be true? A piece of smoked duck hasn't passed my lips for more than seven years. And as for peacock heart! Well, I never! Such delicacies for the likes of her—a thief!"

"She's not a thief. And you won't smell any of the peacock heart. It's all hers. My sister needs the strength! Here! Take some duck and these cakes and grapes and be silent."

"Hmm! Strong words from an urchin. Where are your manners? Did your mother not teach you to respect your elders? Where have you learned to be so commanding? Are you sure you're just a peasant boy? Come closer to the front of my gate so I can see you. My eyes have grown dim in here."

Kiya pushed some parcels though the bars of the woman's gate. "If you want the food, take it now. Or the offer no longer stands."

"You don't fool me. You're not who you say you are! Doesn't help, though . . . being grand and yet having no one to save you! Very well. I'll take it and sit in a corner and do as I'm told. I've got used to taking orders these seven years."

Kiya turned to me. "At last! Hurry, Ta-Miu. Eat while I tell you the news. Tuthmosis is back!"

"*Tuthmosis!* What? Who told you?"

"They say he's here in Thebes and that girl is with him."

"The girl? The girl he escaped with? Isikara?"

"Yes, the same one. The daughter of the embalmer at the temple of the crocodile god, Sobek."

"Why have they returned?"

"No one knows, but the palace is in turmoil. There are guards everywhere. That's why I couldn't come before."

"What about Samut? Why hasn't *he* come?"

Kiya pulled at a loose strand of her wig. "No one has seen Samut for days. I've asked my serving girls for news of him. They say he's disappeared."

I reached through the bars and grabbed hold of her arm. "He *can't* have. If he's left Thebes, how will I be freed? Who will speak out for me?"

"Ta-Miu, believe me, Samut's not to be trusted. He's the tomb robber. The ring is proof of that. But he wants you and Tuthmosis to take the blame. If that's what Wosret believes, why should Samut confess?"

"But I'm completely innocent. Surely he'll confess to giving me the ring?"

Kiya kept silent.

I shook the bars. "Don't you believe I'm innocent?"

She twitched her shoulders. "Of course I do. But others don't."

"Samut *must* speak up for me."

"And ruin his life? Why should he?"

"Because . . . because . . ."

Kiya stared back at me.

I stamped my foot. "What? What are you looking at?"

She kept silent.

"Then *why* did he give me the ring?"

"Ta-Miu, stop protecting Samut. He's deserted you. You must speak out against him. It's your only chance to free yourself. You *have* to, Ta-Miu. You have to confess he was the tomb robber."

"Not until he tells me so himself."

"Then, you'll *never* leave here." She put her hand through the bars and touched my shoulder. "We both fell for his charm."

"But why has he deserted me?" Our eyes met. She seemed more grown-up. Our roles had been reversed. She was now my comforter. "Can't you plead with Amenhotep?" I asked.

She shook her head. "There's been no chance.

Everything is in an uproar since the news came out. Secrets and rumors are flying about. Nefertiti is anxious. She's scared the throne will be taken from Amenhotep. She'll lose her position."

"So what's to be done about me?"

"You know the truth. You know Tuthmosis didn't rob his father's tomb. You know he left Thebes without a single jewel. You were the only one who saw him leave that night. Everyone else was at the temple celebrating Sophet and the rising of the Great River. You were the one who helped find a boat. You helped them escape. You know what was in the boat."

"It's true."

"Then speak out, Ta-Miu. Tell the truth. Confess to Wosret that Samut was the tomb robber. Clear yourself."

I stepped back from the gate beyond her reach. "You make it sound so easy. But I cannot! Tomb robbers are put to death."

"You must!"

"I can't. He's my friend."

"Tuthmosis is a truer friend."

I blocked my ears. "Stop this, Kiya! I can't speak out against Samut."

I couldn't. We'd whispered stories to each other. He'd said he was a tomb robber. But he'd been joking. It couldn't be true. And yet . . . No! He couldn't have done something so dreadful. Of *course* he'd been joking.

I would never speak out against Samut. Never!

13

WOSRET

The night was sultry and dark. The face of the moon god, Khonsu, had dipped toward the west and lost its brightness in a layer of dust that clung to the horizon. The hot night wind blowing in from the desert had brought so much dust that even the stars were dulled and the night murky.

Wosret's skin felt sticky with sweat. A fine layer of grit had settled on him.

The streets of Thebes were empty. Except for the

dry rattle of palm leaves and the rasp of stray pieces of reed scraping against the dirt as they blew down the road, the street was silent. A rat scuttling out suddenly from beneath a bundle of reeds startled him.

Wosret turned into a side alley, where a single dog nosed around some discarded bones, cracking them in his teeth. The sound echoed in the silence. Every now and again the dog stood with his head alert as if expecting a hyena or desert jackal to slink into his territory. As Wosret approached, the dog loped off toward the outskirts of the town to sniff out an unwary rat where the mud houses and alleyways gave way to the desert. In the darkness the dog's outline soon blurred.

Wosret walked between the shadows of the sphinxes toward the new Southern Opet Temple. He'd chosen the temple with purpose. If someone entered by chance, they'd not be surprised to find a priest there. Yet still he'd taken the precaution of covering his shaved head and priestly garments with a cloak.

His stomach grumbled. The hour was late, and the leg of venison he'd dined on and the goblets of good wine he'd drunk had long been digested. The kitchen fires had died down and there was nothing to be had out on the empty streets at this late hour. If only he had had another helping of antelope.

He passed through the huge pylon gates with their mammoth cedar posts and flapping pennants and the towering statue of the old king. The king's eyes stared blankly past him across the gilded paving and over the gardens that were still being laid out all the way down toward the banks of the Great River, where the moon was hovering.

Wosret entered the gilded colonnade with its pairs of papyrus-scroll-shaped columns and searched the shadows for the person he was supposed to meet.

There was a smell of dust and damp pigment in the air. Carvings and inscriptions along the walls were still being worked, and scenes were still being painted. King Amenhotep had hoped to have them completed during his reign. But his death had been sudden. Now it was Wosret's job to see they were finished according to what the king had planned. King Amenhotep leading military expeditions in his chariot. King Amenhotep conquering his enemies. King Amenhotep receiving gifts of gold and ivory from his dominions.

And now of course the new, *young* Amenhotep would want to be included as well, even though he had barely begun to shave! And then there was Nefertiti! Wosret sighed. What a headstrong girl she was becoming! She would want an *entire* wall of carvings devoted to her.

Yes . . . she showed all the signs of being a determined and *very* demanding young woman. His work would be cut out for him, trying to direct her. She was as strong-willed as a camel that had just smelled water and was dead set on reaching it. Ruling Egypt as the first royal wife meant everything to her.

He scrutinized the new carvings in the dim light. Then scowled.

Could it be? Was that *small* figure carrying Amun's barge a depiction of himself? He went up to get a closer look. Was this how he was to be seen by the world? He frowned up at the figure of King Amenhotep, who strode beside him like a colossus.

In the morning he would order the carvers to enlarge his own figure. It was true a king should tower over all his subjects and his enemies, but there was no need for the highest of high priests to *cower* beneath the armpits of a king. A bit of height was needed to add stature.

At the end of the colonnade, Wosret bowed before the seated statues of the god Amun and his wife, Mut. It had been his idea to install all three of the Theban triad—not just Amun and Mut but also their son Khonsu—in the new temple.

He hurried beyond the colonnade into the vast paved Great Sun Court of King Amenhotep and swept his eyes impatiently around the open space.

Where was this fellow he was supposed to meet? The hour was late! He began to regret his decision. The message had been secretly delivered. Pushed under his door in the middle of the night. The person hadn't left his name. He'd merely said he had a secret to exchange—important news—and had asked to meet in a place and at a time when they would not be seen.

The Great Sun Court was a place where commoners were allowed to enter to celebrate special festivals and to have access to the gods. So to impress the commoners, King Amenhotep had ordered scenes showing people paying homage to their great pharaoh at the Opet Festival, when Amun's golden statue was carried between the two temples of Thebes.

Wosret nodded. Yes, this was exactly the way it

should be. Amun must be celebrated in the darkest recess of the holiest of holy places, in the inner sanctum, where only *he*, Wosret, and the king and a few selected priests could enter . . . away from the eyes of the common people.

But now he was impatient. He wanted his bed, or some food at least. But the daily offering tables had been cleared by the priests. There was not a scrap left to be eaten. And even if a loaf of bread had been forgotten, the mice would've demolished it by now. All that was left were a few lone strands of lotus flowers lying limply against the stone altar, giving off a heady perfume.

Where *was* this fellow? Why was he so tardy? Did he not know that one didn't keep the highest of high priests waiting?

Wosret passed into the utter darkness of the hypostyle hall, with its tall rows of columns that held up the solid stone slabs spanning the roof. Not a vestige of Khonsu's moonlight entered here. Two oil lamps were burning in some niches next to the small chambers dedicated to Mut and Khonsu.

He removed one and entered a small chamber to the west. The moon god, Khonsu, stood tall and upright in the flickering light, with the full moon disk resting in the cup of a crescent moon on his head, and a sickle-shaped moon pectoral across his chest. His sacred baboon was at his feet, and in his hands he held the crook and flail of Horus.

Wosret bowed. He might as well gain favor. An extra prayer might reap rewards. So he began intoning, "I built this house for thee, Khonsu, god of rebirth, god of the moon, and lined its doorposts and doors with gold, to look like the horizon of heaven. I decorated the walls with your image being carried on your sacred barge, with its falcon's head at the prow during your special festival, when the birth of the New Year is celebrated. Look down now on your humble servant and grant my request that Nefertiti will soon give birth."

It was right to make this request. In a few more nights Khonsu's face would turn away and the new moon would hang, as thin as a nail paring, in the sky. Everyone knew the time of the new moon was a time of rebirth, when Khonsu allowed women to conceive.

Nefertiti needed a baby son to keep her occupied and less troublesome.

An echo of footsteps made him turn. A figure stood in the doorway of Khonsu's chamber. He had pulled a cloak across his face.

Wosret narrowed his eyes. "Speak your name, fellow."

"The information I give, sir, has no need of a name."

Wosret glanced beyond the man into the shadows. "How can I be sure you weren't followed?"

"I'm no stranger to the need for vigilance."

"Drop your cloak, then, so I can see you're unarmed."

As he did so, Wosret held up the lamp and tried to recall where he had seen the young man's face before. "Do I know you?"

The young man shook his head. "We don't attend the same places."

Wosret studied him carefully. "How can you be sure I want this information?"

The young man held his look. "You wouldn't be here otherwise."

Wosret sighed heavily. "Get on with it, then. But not under the eyes of Khonsu. Go through the doorway into the room ahead that has the barge of Amun.

You must swear on the holy barge that you speak the truth."

Wosret held the lamp up to light the way. The young man's shoulders were broad and muscled. He had the confident air of someone not used to being subservient.

They stood in the small stuffy chamber that enclosed Amun's barge. Wosret nodded. "Get on with it, then. What do you need to tell me? And what favor do you want of me?"

In the lamplight Wosret saw the young man arch an eyebrow. "I've no favor to ask, but a man never knows when one will be needed."

"That's true. Place your hand on Amun's sacred barge and say what you have to say. I'm in a hurry to be home."

The young man stretched out a hand to touch the gold of the sacred barge but didn't take his eyes from Wosret's face. "Tuthmosis has returned to Thebes. He has come to claim his kingship back from his brother."

Wosret gave him a dark look. "Is that *all* you have to say? Do you think I don't know? You kept me from my bed to tell me *this*!"

"You might know he has returned, but you don't know Tuthmosis's exact whereabouts. I do."

"How so?"

"He's disguised."

"Then, how do you know it's truly him?"

"I know his face and his blue eyes. He's in the Place of Maat. The girl, Isikara, the one he escaped with, is there as well. They're staying in different places, but I know the exact houses where they're hiding."

14

THE PRISON—
TA-MIU

Treachery is difficult to live with. It's a viper that rises up unexpectedly from the desert sands and strikes when you least expect it. The spells of the afterlife ask the heart not to be treacherous or disloyal.

But Samut had been both. Why had he deserted me? How could I live with such disloyalty? It caught me by my throat. I was foolish to have believed him.

Yet who was more treacherous? I, for betraying

the secret of the duplicate key? Or Samut, for acting on it?

A mouse scuttled out from some straw beneath my pallet. Its sharp eyes peeped at me. Then it disappeared. I was lonelier with it gone.

"That boy wasn't your brother, was he?"

I kept my lips shut tight. Why did the old woman want so many answers?

"Don't feel like speaking today? Well, see if I'm bothered. Don't think I'll be bowing and scraping to you just because you think you're important enough to have smoked duck and peacock hearts brought to you. The smoked duck wasn't as tasty as it should've been. Dried out and overcooked. And not even a drop of wine to wash it down with!"

I gripped the ankh and began gouging at the walls again.

Samut had shown me the palace chariot house and the stables, with their stone water basins and their sloping floors and troughs at the lower end for keeping the floor as dry as possible and for catching the horses' urine. We went on a night when the moon god, Khonsu, was showing just a sliver of his face. Our path through the palace gardens was dark and silent. We timed the guards' movements and waited for the stable boy to go off with one of the maids.

What a noise the horses made when they heard Samut's voice! He called them with sounds through his teeth and spoke in low murmurs that weren't proper words. They answered with snorts and whinnies and stamps of their hooves.

I worried the noise would bring the guards running and wake everyone in the palace. But Samut went up and down the stalls talking to each one, rubbing across the bridges of their noses, blowing into their faces and stroking their flanks while the horses nuzzled his neck and tossed their heads and arched their swan necks and tried to push their way out of each stall to get closer to him even though they were tethered.

He had the same manner with horses as the horsemen who had brought Kiya and me to Egypt from Mitanni. But even those horsemen had never received as much attention from their horses as these ones gave Samut.

"They're not war horses. They're hunting horses," he told me, "trained to chase across the desert weaving back and forth after the swiftest antelope or cheetah, pulling marksmen in chariots behind them."

I nodded. "I know. In Mitanni we called them wind-eaters. Horses that run swifter than the wind. Running fast enough to swallow it."

"The old king's two favorite stallions are here. Come and see," he said, and took my hand.

I gazed at Maarqada, a horse as black as the night, with fearless eyes, and Mimreh, a dark bay with a proud strong neck.

"They wore duplicates of King Amenhotep's chest pectorals and the leopard cloak of honor across their backs when they pulled his chariot. Now Amenhotep the son has claimed them along with the milk white Assyrian horses. Nefertiti, too, has been given a pair of chestnut stallions for her own chariot."

He spread his hands for me to see. "This is where my scars come from. I worked here as a boy."

So he was not a falconer. Nor was he a tomb robber.

That's why he'd brought me there. That's why he knew so much about the horses and why he'd known how to bind my leg. He had bound sprained ankles—or rather sprained fetlocks.

"My father was chief vizier of the stables. King Amenhotep sent envoys to your country to find the very best horse trainer to make sure his horses were the fastest, strongest, and finest-bred horses ever seen. The trainer worked them until he knew the precise moment when each horse was both physically and instinctively ready for what lay ahead. He didn't want to risk his own life by having the king thrown out of his chariot because of a badly trained horse!

"He used unusual methods. Instead of putting them behind a chariot, he made them trot and canter over exactly marked distances for long periods until their muscles were strong and lean. He identified horses with breathing problems by blocking all the cracks in the stable walls to increase dust and mold. Any horse with the slightest chest problem was rejected."

All this Samut reported as we passed through the stables stall by stall. He interrupted himself to pause and murmur to each individual horse and call it by its name.

I said nothing but walked with my hand twined in his. I knew about horses. I'm a daughter of a horseman, after all. I came from the Khābūr Mountains. My father's father and his father before him and my brothers were all horsemen. It's in my blood.

We came to the room where the chariots and harnesses and fodder were stored. A strong smell of leather and straw and newly shaved wood hung in the air.

"Sit here, Ta-Miu," he said.

A stray stable cat came and purred up against us. And Samut traced lightly over the cat tattoo on my shoulder. I felt his breath against my neck. I saw myself reflected in his eyes. He touched the two cords about my neck and held first the glass scarab and then the ankh in turn. His skin smelled of straw and leather and the sweet-sour smell of horses.

"Whose heart does the ankh open?" he whispered.

I shook my head. "It's just a key."

"Just a key?"

I pressed my fingers to his lips to stop him from asking further.

"But what key? A key to what?"

"If I tell you, will you never speak of it again?"

He nodded. "I promise."

"It's a key to a gate. The gate guards the secret entry from the palace gardens into the king's labyrinth and his burial chambers."

"King Amenhotep's burial chambers?"

I nodded and saw my face reflected in Samut's eyes.

And then I told him about the other key. The duplicate one hidden on a shelf just within the gate.

So who was the more treacherous? Samut or I?

15

BETRAYAL AT THE PLACE OF MAAT

The silence of the room was broken by the scratch of Tuthmosis's stylus against papyrus.

Outside in the street, children were playing rhyming games, and some boys were batting a reed ball with a stick and shouting at their brothers to catch. The walls were papyrus-thin. Someone in the next-door house was scolding a child for allowing the dog inside. A sound of chopping and an aroma of chickpeas and onions and smells of roasted pigeon came drifting to him. Hera's mother was preparing the evening meal.

In a niche above him a statue of Bes, the household god, was dancing and banging his cymbals to frighten away evils. Tuthmosis touched the statue for good luck. He knew by the slant of sun entering the high west window at the top of the room that it was almost time for the workers to come back from their day shift. Hera was right. The village was a skeleton that lost all its flesh and muscle and brawn by daylight. Soon the front door would be flung open. He'd have to hide in the hot, stuffy cellar again while Hera's boisterous brothers ate supper and drank their daily ration of beer with their neighbors. When the village settled down for the night, he'd come out and sleep with the family on mats on the rooftop under the stars, where the side walls screened him from inquisitive neighbors.

But now he was anxious for Hera to come home. He needed to get the message to Amenhotep. Every now and again the point of his stylus caught against an uneven bump of papyrus and sent a spray of sooty ink over the surface. When the final word was written, he blew hurriedly across the surface to dry the ink before he rolled the papyrus and dropped a blob of warm wax across the edge. Then he turned his ring and pressed its seal into the wax.

Amenhotep would recognize the seal. When he broke it and read what was written, he'd *have* to believe Tuthmosis.

Hera would make sure the seal wasn't broken by the wrong person. He had promised it would be delivered into the king's own hands. Tuthmosis had warned Hera, "The letter will contain every detail of Wosret's plot to take over Egypt. All he has done to wrong me. If Wosret gets hold of it before my brother, I won't stand a chance. My throat will be slit before I can prove myself."

Hera had given his word. "I swear I'll give it to one of the king's own bedchamber attendants. I've been painting the wings of the vulture goddess in his chamber. Amenhotep comes daily to inspect the work. Perhaps I'll see him break the seal."

"Whatever happens, you *must* be vigilant. My life's at stake. Wosret won't allow his plans to be stopped again. He wants me out of the way."

"Trust me! How long have you known me, Tut? I'll make sure the letter gets to your brother. I won't forget what you did for me. When I was only an apprentice mixing pigments in your father's tomb, you had me promoted. You have my word. I won't fail you."

As Tuthmosis withdrew his sealing ring from the wax, he heard angry shouts. Hera's mother came rushing from the back room and heaved herself breathlessly up the steps to the open rooftop.

"Come quickly!" she panted as she passed him. "But don't allow yourself to be seen."

They crouched below the low wall that rimmed the rooftop and peered down into the roadway below. Some men were banging on the door of a house a few paces away. It was the house where Isikara was staying.

Before Tuthmosis could do anything, she was dragged out into the road.

"Leave me be! I work in this village," she shouted as she fought to get away from the man holding her.

"Then, show us your papers that say you are registered here."

"Papers? Hah! Who among you can even read?"

Tuthmosis clenched his fists. *Don't, Isikara! Don't make it worse for yourself! Just keep silent!*

"She was led into a trap!" Hera's mother whispered. "Listen to what the women down there are saying. It was a ruse. A child knocked on her door and said she was ill and needed water. Isikara took pity on her and let her in."

"Where was your sister? Why didn't she answer the door?"

"It's her day for temple duty. She's gone to Thebes."

The men had tied Isikara's hands behind her back and were hoisting her onto a donkey. Tuthmosis slammed his fist into the palm of his hand. "I can't just stand by and watch."

"Are you stupid?" Hera's mother grabbed him by the shoulder and yanked him back. "You'd get arrested yourself." Her chest heaved as she pushed him down below the wall again.

Tuthmosis tried to shrug her off. "I have to! I can't leave her to those thugs."

"Listen to me! Six soldiers against *one*? What madness! Wait for my sons to return. They'll be here soon. They'll get her back. Trust me."

"But who betrayed her? Your sister?"

"My *sister*?" Hera's mother glared at him. She looked as if she wanted to give him a good clout across the head. "The blood that runs through our family is as true and pure as any that runs through royalty. My sister's honor is beyond doubt. She'd never break a promise. She'd *never* reveal the whereabouts of someone she'd promised to hide."

"Who, then? Who gave her away?"

She pointed. "That hyena skulking over there. You can be sure it was him. Doesn't do a day's work yet always has enough food and beer. If there's work to be done, don't look to him. I should've sued him the day he sold me that lame donkey for a pot of fat. I hope the fat went rancid on him."

Tuthmosis peered out to where Hera's mother was pointing. His breath caught. Of all the people who could have been standing there . . . of all the people who could have given Isikara's hiding place away . . . the water carriers, the potters, the stonemasons, the chariot makers, or any other of the workmen from the Place of Maat . . . it was the one person he'd *least* expected.

One whom he hadn't seen since his childhood.

But *why* had he betrayed Isikara?

Tuthmosis saw the boy exchange glances with one of the soldiers and then turn and look deliberately at the house of Hera's family and give a small but definite nod.

So he knew!

"Quick! You have to make a run for it!" Hera's mother whispered. "Go out through the kitchen into the alleyway at the back and enter the third door on your left. It's my cousin's house. Hide there until all is quiet again. Hurry! Third on the left. Take your papyrus with you. I'll deal with the likes of *him*." She spat down into the street below.

16

THE PRISON— ISIKARA

A noise woke me from a dream of peacocks and high mountains with icy streams. There were horsemen, hundreds of them, and a woman was tugging at me. But then there was a noise of shouting and cursing and feet scuffling along the stone passage.

"You have no right to lock me up! I demand to speak to someone in authority. Who has given the order to take me prisoner? Let go of me!"

It was a girl's voice but not Kiya's . . . followed by a guard bellowing, "Ouch! A pestilence of flies on you! You bit me, you little vixen! May you rot here until your heart is scattered in the Field of Reeds!" Then the sound of a blow. A flat hand hitting against flesh.

"You dog! Do you have *no* feelings? Would you beat your sister like that?"

"If you *were* my sister, I'd have you beaten for behaving like a vixen."

"If you were my *brother*, I'd pray your heart would be carried off by Ammut, devourer of the dead, to the Lake of Fire! Your heart is *already* dead!"

"And yours will soon be too! Get into that cell with that other wretched girl."

"Well, I'm no wretched girl! Take your hands off me! I am Isikara, daughter of the priest at the temple of the crocodile god, Sobek."

Isikara? I pushed myself up hurriedly from my sleeping pallet. Was it really her?

"Not anymore!" the guard sneered. "We all know what happened to your father. He was a traitor, and he got what traitors deserve. And you are no less a traitor."

"May Sobek crunch your bones between his teeth, and may the wind scatter their grit over the desert!"

"You've no power to invoke Sobek!"

"Hah! You forget I was my father's helper at the Temple of Sobek. Who do you think fed and watered the sacred crocodiles and helped with their embalming? Of all people, I've the *most* power in the kingdom to invoke Sobek! Be careful of my curses."

"Wretched girl! You deserve worse than this cell. If you were my sister, I'd have you not just beaten but put to *death*! A mouth as vicious as yours needs to be silenced."

She sprawled against the floor as he shoved her in alongside me. He banged the gate shut, jammed the bolt, and snapped the lock.

She leaped up and grabbed hold of the bars and hissed through them. "And if you were my brother, I'd push you into the crocodile enclosure! You deserve no better than to be eaten by a crocodile," she shouted after his echoing footsteps.

"A fine performance, deary!" the old woman from next door cackled. "But it won't get you far. The best is gotten from them by playing the girlish role. Flirting a little and playing up to their fragile egos."

"I don't care about fragile egos and girlish roles. I've fought side by side with the Nubians. I know about war and battles."

I peered at her. Blood was seeping from a cut on her cheek. Her tunic was ripped and filthy. Her head was completely shaved. "Isikara? Is that you?"

Her eyes raked across me. "Who are *you*?"

"Don't you remember me? It's Ta-Miu. I helped you and Tuthmosis escape from the palace. So it's true, then. You've returned. Where's Tuthmosis? Is he safe?"

Her eyes still flared with tiny stars of anger. "They captured me. I don't know what happened to him."

"I hardly recognized you."

She wiped the blood on her cheek with the back of her hand. "It's me, all the same. My time spent in a Medjay camp and then training with a bow in the sun beside Nubian bowmen would change anyone. You don't exactly look the same either."

"I've been in prison a long time. I'm not sure how long."

"Only seven *days*, deary! I've marked it off. You still have a long way to go before you catch up with my seven *years*!"

Isikara's eyebrows shot up. She inclined her head toward the cell next door. "Does she always listen in?"

I nodded.

She glared around the cramped space. Gave an impatient twitch of her shoulders. "I must get out of here as quickly as possible."

I eyed her. "Do you think I haven't been trying? It's impossible."

"You must speak out. For all I know they might have captured Tuthmosis by now."

"Speak out?" I glanced at her. How much did she know?

She nodded. "In the Place of Maat they say a boy gave you the ring."

I twisted a piece of my tunic between my fingers. "What if he did? It was a copy of the real ring."

She shook her head.

I gave her a hard look. "Are you saying I'm a liar?

"The jeweler who made the ring lives in the Place of Maat. He was arrested and asked to examine it. He swore it was King Amenhotep's original ring. It has the jeweler's mark stamped into the gold. And the original is missing from the king's tomb, so no further evidence is needed. The ring you were given is the real one that belonged to the king."

"May a frog lodge in your throat!" I snapped. "That ring *wasn't* the real one."

"You know I speak the truth. You *have* to tell Wosret who gave it to you."

"I don't have to tell Wosret anything! And I don't have to listen to you! Why should I?"

"A confession is our only chance of getting out. We're *both* accused of helping Tuthmosis escape. Tomb robbers are put to death. Tuthmosis will be put to death if Wosret convinces Amenhotep and Nefertiti that he committed the robbery."

"There's nothing I have to say."

"Ta-Miu, listen to me. Tuthmosis was once your special friend. He's mine as well. Do you *want* him to die?"

"Amenhotep would never send his brother to his death." I blocked my ears. "I don't want to listen. Share my cell if you must. The fleas and lice will soon get to you. But stay away from me!" I flung myself facedown onto the filthy pallet and tucked my arms over my head so I didn't have to hear her.

For a while there was silence except for the old

woman's snoring. I raised my head slightly to see what Isikara was up to.

She was crouched on the stone floor staring ahead of her. Then I saw what she was staring at. She was reading the words I'd carved into the walls.

I jumped up and spread my arms across them. "By all that's holy, don't you *dare*! These are my private thoughts!"

Her eyes turned briefly to me and then went back to the words.

"I said *stop!*"

She ignored me.

I stumbled across the floor, grabbed the ankh, and began scratching through the words. "You have no right. They're not meant for your eyes."

"Who are they for, then? If you write words, you have to be prepared for people to read them."

I spun around to face her. "What do *you* know? I thought I'd die here, and then what did it matter who read them? They're random words. They don't tell the whole story."

"Then, why did you write them?"

"I was trying to discover the truth in my head."

"Have you?"

I clenched the ankh in my fist. Stared straight back at her.

She didn't turn away. "Will the boy who stole the ring, the one you wrote of . . . the boy you told the secret to . . . Will he come for you?"

"A pestilence of flies on you! You read everything!"

"Everything . . . except you didn't write his name. Who is he?"

"Do you think I'd tell you?"

"You have to, if we're to escape."

"A curse on you for prying!" I flung the ankh at her. It missed her head, hit the wall behind, and fell to the floor. *"You!"*

She picked it up calmly and stared back at me, her eyes like emeralds flecked with particles of gold dust in the half-light. "Yes?"

"You left Thebes. Now you think you can come back and tell me what I should do. I wish I'd never helped you escape with Tuthmosis. How dare you judge me? You know nothing about what's been happening. *Nothing* at all!" I spat out the words.

"I know how evil Wosret is."

"How would you? You've not been here in Thebes!"

"Wosret's power extends beyond Thebes. I can

prove it!" She thrust out her right hand. "They took off my bow fingers in Nubia."

I shrunk back from the two fingers that ended abruptly at the second knuckle. The scars were red and raw and horrible to look at.

"The Nubians?"

She shook her head. "The Egyptians." Then she changed the subject. "So you told that boy a secret?"

"What if I did?"

"You told him about the key Tuthmosis gave you. The key to the labyrinth. Didn't you?"

"You're guessing. My words don't say that."

"But they say you told him a *secret* you shouldn't have told."

I stared back at her.

"He's the tomb robber, isn't he?"

"You don't know that for *certain*. Besides, I didn't give him the key." I snatched the ankh from her hand and held it up. "*This* key I'm holding, *this* is the one Tuthmosis gave me! See, I still have it!"

She nodded. "I know you didn't give the boy *that* key."

"Then, how can you accuse me?"

"You didn't have to give the boy your own key.

You told him where to find the *other* key. The duplicate one that lay on the ledge inside the gate."

"What? How do you know there's a second key?"

"You've forgotten. I escaped the labyrinth with Tuthmosis using that exact key. It's on the ledge next to the gate, where it's always kept. Your friend—the one whose name you're careful not to mention—used it to enter the secret gate to King Amenhotep's tomb."

She held my look. "You told him it was there. *He's* the tomb robber. Speak out against him."

I wanted to spring forward and tear out her throat. But the lioness spirit of Sekhmet failed me. Instead I jabbed my ankh hard into the surface of the wall. "Stay away from me," I spat. "You're asking me to betray someone I love. Betrayal is the worst form of treachery."

"No, I'm asking you to protect someone who was once your friend. Tuthmosis is worth defending. If you don't defend him, you betray *his* trust in you. Who is more worth defending . . . Tuthmosis or this other boy?"

17

LADY OF FLAME

K iya paced back and forth, twisting the edge of her sleeve between her fingers. She couldn't gather her thoughts. They darted about like fireflies in her head. Tiny, bright thoughts zigzagging back and forth but going nowhere.

How would she rescue Ta-Miu?

A maid sighed and nodded in her direction. "What's to be done? Just look at what she's doing to that cloth. She'll tear it to shreds, and then *we'll* have to mend it."

"Do you think we should find her a second chameleon to distract her?"

The other maid shrugged. "Nothing will distract her until Ta-Miu is free."

"Hah! Well, she'll wear out her sandals on that one. Ta-Miu's not worth fretting about. She got what she deserves."

"How so?"

"She stole the ring!"

"You don't know for sure. I smell a dead fish. I don't think the tomb robbery has anything to do with Ta-Miu. She's not the sort who would do something as shocking as steal from a tomb. I think she's innocent."

"Innocent? A girl who runs off every afternoon to meet a boy and leaves us to do all her work . . . *innocent*? Hah! And if she's so innocent, why's she in prison?"

"It was *you*, wasn't it? You told about the ring being under her bedclothes?"

"What if I did? She's the guilty one. She's the one who's in prison."

"Just because someone's in prison doesn't make them *guilty!*" The maid reached out her hand to Kiya. "My lady, please stop! All that tearing at your sleeve won't return Ta-Miu to us."

Kiya looked back blankly at her and then went on pacing.

Whom could she appeal to? It would be useless to plead with Nefertiti. It suited her to have Ta-Miu accused of stealing the ring with Tuthmosis. Nefertiti was terrified he'd come to claim his throne. She'd want to blame Tuthmosis. To have Ta-Miu accused of treachery as well made her argument against Tuthmosis all the stronger. And Wosret was aligned with Nefertiti.

Who, then? There was only Amenhotep.

She snapped her fingers and swung around. "Prepare a fresh robe. I must speak to the king."

"What will you say, my lady?"

Kiya flopped down onto her bed. "Yes, what *will* I say? Oh, Hathor, protector of women, help me. What must I say to Amenhotep? If only Ta-Miu were here to help me!"

"It's not Hathor you need now, my lady. It's her opposite fighting spirit, Sekhmet, you must call on. The lioness goddess, Sekhmet, will rise up and claw your enemies by the throat. I urge you. Call on her, rather than Hathor, to strike at your enemies."

Kiya sighed from her curled-up position on the bed. "Yes, you're right."

"Sekhmet removes every threat. She punishes all who wrong Maat. Implore her, the lioness, the Lady of Flame, to be on your side when you speak to Amenhotep. Come, get up now! Wear your gilded silver pectoral inlaid with lapis lazuli and agate and your lioness amulet of gold to protect you."

"Yes." Kiya jumped from the bed. "You're right. I'll wear the pectoral and the amulet. I'll call on Sekhmet, the Lady of Flame, to stand alongside me in her flame red dress stained with the blood of her foes. I'll ask her to breathe on my enemies with the hot desert wind of her breath! Prepare my robe. I'll wear the one threaded with red as well. Nefertiti will *not* dictate what I can or cannot wear tonight. With Sekhmet at my side I'll show my fighting spirit."

Then the maid leaned forward and whispered into her ear, "Remember too that the king is young and still a boy. Don't be too fiery. Beguile him with your own young and charming ways, Princess Tadukhepa. Keep Hathor at your side as well."

✦ ✦ ✦

Despite her bravery while she was bathing and preparing to see Amenhotep, now, as she stood waiting for him in the antechamber to his private quarters, Kiya felt nervous. How would he receive her? What if Nefertiti, the very person she most dreaded, accompanied him? She regretted the flamboyance of her red woven dress. And she wasn't sure of the rules. Was it necessary to remove her sandals in the presence of the king?

The grandeur of the chambers made her wish she hadn't come alone. Some attendants would have given her courage. The person she truly needed at her side was Ta-Miu. Yet she was the very reason she was here.

Everything in the king's quarters was grand and lavish. The walls, painted the deepest blue, as dark as the night, seemed made of lapis lazuli and were embellished with gold stars. And hovering across the ceiling was the vulture goddess, Nekhbet. Her huge outstretched wings were inlaid with gold, turquoise, and carnelian. And in each of the four corners of the room, a flaring golden cobra with ruby eyes rose up ready to strike at the king's enemies. On the snake's heads were gold sun disks. Tongues of fire flickered out from them.

Kiya closed her eyes. The splendor was making her dizzy.

Someone touched her shoulder. A fragrance of cinnamon and sandalwood wafted toward her. She snapped open her eyes again.

Amenhotep was standing in front of her. By contrast to the magnificence of the room, he wore a simply tied white linen wrap, and his head was unadorned by either a crown or even a wig. He was unattended, and his short hair was tousled and wet and dripped down onto his shoulders. He stood in front of her, looking as casual and disheveled as if he'd just come from swimming with friends in the river. Without his fine robes and leopard cloak and the double Atef crown or his blue warrior crown, he seemed just an ordinary young, handsome boy.

She dropped her eyes in confusion.

Amenhotep laughed. "What were you dreaming?"

Kiya looked back up at him. Now it was his turn to glance away quickly. Perhaps he was shy. She suddenly remembered she should bow. "I wasn't dreaming, my lord. I was in fact dizzy."

"Dizzy? Are you ill?"

She shook her head. "No . . . confused rather."

"Confused?"

"I don't know what to do," she blurted out, and then was vexed for sounding like a child.

"About what?"

By all that was holy, she truly wished Ta-Miu were with her. She felt stupid for gabbling. "I implore you to bring Ta-Miu back to the palace. I can't cope without her."

"But you have so many maids."

She gave him a quick look. Was he laughing at her? She shook her head. "It's not her services I need. It's her good advice."

"Good advice?" He raised an eyebrow. "From a tomb robber?"

Surely he was teasing her. She shook her head vigorously. "You can't believe she robbed your father's tomb?" She wrinkled her nose in frustration. A pestilence! Now she'd spoken too freely again!

"Who did, then?"

She bit her lip. It had been on the tip of her tongue to blurt out Samut's name. "I can't say. But I beg you to be kind until this is resolved. The prison is a terrible place."

"How would you know?"

What would he say if she told him that she'd visited Ta-Miu disguised as her brother? She rushed on before she could make any more mistakes. "Please allow her to return to the palace."

He pulled a face. "Nefertiti won't be happy."

"If Ta-Miu can't return as my maid, allow her at least to work somewhere in the palace. She'll die in prison. Let her work in the weaving rooms, or in the unguent rooms or the wig workshops. There must be *some* position that needs to be filled."

He laughed as if he knew he shouldn't be laughing. "Nefertiti won't take kindly to Ta-Miu being freed. It has to be something that keeps her out of sight."

"So you *will* free her, then?" Without thinking, Kiya took hold of Amenhotep's hands. Then suddenly realized what she'd done. She felt the color rise in her cheeks as she fell into a bow. "Forgive me."

But Amenhotep helped her up firmly. It was odd. He had a strength that came from the quiet way he held himself. He didn't blurt out words like she did.

"What work shall I give her? Should I send her to the potteries? She could learn to make floor tiles and decorate them. Would that suit you?"

Kiya bit her lip. "The potteries are no place for

a girl. The work is hard, the clay rough, and the heat of the kilns unbearable. Isn't there something gentler she can do?"

"What about the unguent rooms? She'd be surrounded by lilies and roses and exotic scents and flagons of precious oils." He seemed unsure of himself and let go of her hands. "Girls like that, don't they?"

"Perhaps Isikara can be sent as well. I've heard she has also been imprisoned."

He shrugged. "There can't be any harm. The unguent rooms are as safe as any prison."

Kiya remembered to bow. "You're very kind."

"I watched you and Ta-Miu when Tuthmosis was showing off with his throwing stick and his archery skills. I was jealous of Tuthmosis. When Tuthmosis had his accident and his leg was broken and wouldn't heal, I hoped he'd die." Amenhotep hesitated. "And then it happened—or so I was led to believe by Wosret. Finally he *was* dead! And I was filled with guilt because I thought I'd brought on his death by my wishes."

She smiled. "Well, you are free of your guilt now. Tuthmosis is alive after all."

Amenhotep suddenly frowned. "Yes, but all

Nefertiti has in her head is that he's come to claim his throne. Do you think it's true? The throne is rightfully his. He could claim you back as well."

Kiya bowed. "I'm your obedient servant. My father sent me from Mitanni to Egypt as a gift to the king. The king died, so *you* are now my husband."

"Yes . . . but if Tuthmosis ruled Egypt, would you remain my wife?"

She tried to hide her smile. Her maid had been right. She'd called on the lioness Sekhmet to fight at her side. But it seemed it was Sekhmet's opposite spirit, Hathor, goddess of love, who'd appeared as well this evening.

"I think I might."

PART
THREE

18
NEFERTITI'S CHAMBERS

Nefertiti sat stroking her cheetahs as they lolled across the pillows of her bed. "I've heard that Princess Tadukhepa has visited Amenhotep's chambers. And he was seen reading a note delivered by a secret messenger."

Wosret seemed startled. "A note? I've not heard of a note."

"Well, there was one. It was given to my husband by a servant, who in turn told my servant. The note was sealed. No one had the courage to break the seal and read it before it was delivered. Do you think it was from Princess Tadukhepa?"

"Why would she send the king a note?"

"She's bold. She thinks she can get Amenhotep's attention. She's a scheming little desert fox. I can see it in her eyes even though she tries to appear innocent."

"Don't trouble yourself with her. She's very young. You're the queen, and soon you'll have a child to prove to Egypt how great a queen you are." He bowed his head and said quickly, "May Hathor ensure it's a boy!"

"But she vexes me!" Nefertiti's mouth twitched as she shrugged her shoulders. One of the cheetahs snarled. She turned and fondled its ears absent-mindedly and smoothed out the jeweled chain around its neck. "Wosret, find the note so we can see what she's written."

"The note is probably to ask for forgiveness for her maid."

"Not all that fuss again! The maid's a thief. She deserves to be locked up forever for being in posses-sion of King Amenhotep's emerald ring."

"Your husband, Amenhotep the Younger, thinks you are too rash."

"Too rash?" Nefertiti sat up so abruptly that the cheetahs leaped up from the bed and began stalking around the room. "Too rash, when I've discovered she's secretly visited Amenhotep? And there's a rumor she's sent him a note, and now the rumor that Tuthmosis has returned and is ready to snatch the crown!"

Her agitation made the cheetahs snarl and hiss. Their heavy tails swished behind them. Wosret stepped aside as they paced past him. "Can't you make these infernal animals lie down? They belong in a cage, not stalking around a bedchamber. And certainly not on your bed. They're surely riddled with fleas. Get them to lie down on their pillows."

"They're only doing what cheetahs know to do. They're hunters. So they pace."

"Well, train them to stand still. They make me nervous!"

"I thought nothing made you nervous!" Nefertiti gave a laugh like the sound of her bangles jangling against one another.

Wosret shook his head impatiently. "So you've

heard the rumor. The matter of Tuthmosis is truly *serious*, Nefertiti. It's what I've come to see you about. I've tracked down the girl he ran away with and have had her imprisoned."

"The embalmer's daughter?"

Wosret nodded. "Yes, Isikara. But she's a feisty girl and won't answer questions. And Tuthmosis gave my men the slip. He's gone into hiding and can't be found. There's rumor he wants to meet his brother. We can't let him take the throne. If he does, your position is at stake."

Nefertiti glanced up quickly. "Surely there's a way around this?"

"How?"

"I could become Tuthmosis's wife."

"And leave Amenhotep?"

"You're clever, Wosret. You'll think of something." She took hold of his hand. "You're the highest of high priests, after all. You can arrange anything. Make sure I keep the crown . . . whatever happens."

Wosret made a sound more like a growl than a laugh. "You give me powers beyond my capability."

"But the matter of Tuthmosis must be dealt

with, and dealt with quickly. I *must* remain queen at all costs. Do what you have to. But first I want you to find the note from that Naharin girl. I want to discover what she's written to Amenhotep. There's too much at stake."

19

THE UNGUENT ROOMS

The sound of the old woman's voice woke me.

"Seems you're both important. Here's someone with a bunch of keys to unlock your cell! Oi! Where are you taking them?"

"None of your business, old woman!"

I shook Isikara. "Wake up! We're being released!"

Two guards pulled us past the old woman's cell, and I saw her tired ancient face for the first time. She reached a hand out through the bars to try to snatch at the guards. "What's so important about the likes of *them*? What about *me*?"

"I'll speak out for you, old woman. I promise!" I called back over my shoulder.

We were forced up some steps and marched outside. The brightness and confusion and tumult in the street hurt my eyes. I stumbled and was yanked and trundled along among people who jostled and stared and pointed. The sharp clink of weapons knocking against each other kept me in check.

Across the Great River the Theban hills quivered in the heat. The sun burned hot on my shoulders. We were pushed on board a ferry. Where were they taking us? I avoided Isikara's eyes as we sat on opposite sides of the boat. I was still smarting from her judgment of me.

On the western bank we were put on donkeys and taken to the palace. Once through the gates, we were led away from the path that led to Kiya's quarters and passed into a workshop area. The donkeys halted in a courtyard completely enclosed by mud brick buildings. A strong perfume of roses and lilies filled the hot, dry air.

Isikara nudged me and whispered. "Where are we? Is this another prison?"

I refused to answer, even though I knew we were at the palace unguent rooms.

She kept her voice low. "We must grab the first chance to escape, so you can defend Tuthmosis."

I gave her a sharp look. "Don't be so sure! I haven't promised *anything* yet," I snapped.

The guards spoke to a frail, elderly man. There were deep frown marks on his forehead as he looked in our direction. Then we were left in the courtyard, while the guards rode off on the donkeys and the gates were closed and locked behind them.

The old man stepped up close to peer at us. Then, as he stretched out his hand to touch our faces, I realized he was blind.

"I'm judging your youth and the size of your noses. Only a good strong nose can create fragrances. Apart from a sensitive nose, you need a good memory and an ability to precisely describe scents." He took a step back. "Do you have these qualities?"

It was unnerving, having him stare at me when I knew he couldn't see me. I kept silent. Neither did Isikara answer.

"Hmmph! I thought so!" The old man shook his head wearily. "There was a time when the job of a perfume maker was handed down from father to son, but times have changed. Now they've sent me two completely ignorant prison girls. What must I do with you? What good are you? Noses must be trained to pick up scent, like flypaper picks up flies. You've probably already allowed your sense of smell to be distracted by all sorts of odors. You probably don't know a dead fish from a dead rat!"

I saw Isikara toss her head. "I think I would! I know about dead bodies. I trained as an embalmer."

"Don't answer back. I won't take nonsense. Especially from girls who have no sense of smell."

"Who's to say we have no sense of smell?"

"I say so! Because you both stink. You are an unwashed riot of odors. Nobody knows for sure what makes our noses work the way they do. But yours are clearly not working!"

"It was the prison. We had no access to water," Isikara replied.

"There's a stone trough over there," he said brusquely. "Scrub yourselves down with a paste of ash and clay and put on the clean tunics you'll find hanging there, before you set foot in my unguent rooms."

I sensed Isikara's eyes on me as I walked ahead.

"If we're to escape, we might as well try to be friends, Ta-Miu," she whispered as soon as we were out of earshot.

I dunked my head into a trough of cold water so as not to listen. Then rubbed the paste into my itchy scalp as hard as I could, annoyed that she thought I could be won over so easily.

"Why do you suppose they've brought us here?"

I dunked my head again and then swept the wet hair back from my forehead and gave her a look. "It was probably Kiya's work. But don't think we're *truly* released."

Isikara stopped scrubbing at the dirt under her nails. "Why do you say that?"

"The courtyard has locked gates."

"So?"

"It's kept locked because of the secrets the workshops contain. Recipes for perfume made especially for the palace. And in some cases perfumes for only one person. Queen Tiy had her own secret lily perfume made by the old man himself, and no other. His name is Intef."

"What's that to do with us?" Isikara asked as she

pulled a clean tunic over her head and rearranged the folds.

"Everyone who works here is kept locked up so they can't give out the secrets."

The old man, Intef, suddenly appeared in the doorway. His sight might have been impaired, but his hearing was good. "Your friend is right. Perfume makers are always confined. They're kept under lock and key in this courtyard to protect the secrets of the palace perfumes. Revealing the secrets of the unguent rooms is punishable by death. Now follow me."

I glanced at Isikara to see how she was taking this news. Kiya had freed us from real prison, but this was another sort.

Isikara shrugged. "We must be clever and use every opportunity to our advantage," she whispered, then gave me a shove. "Stop scowling and make yourself pleasant."

I turned on my heel and followed Intef. Who was *she* to tell *me* to look pleasant?

The odors in the first room were overwhelming. Shafts of sunlight sliced the room into spaces of light and dark. But as my eyes became accustomed, I saw it was a storeroom.

Shelves were piled high with bundles of bark. Bunches of grasses and herbs hung from the ceiling. Wicker trays were piled with dried rose petals. And everywhere there were containers of dark, twisted roots, jars of black berries, flagons of oil, and stone basins that held lumps of amber-colored resin as large as my fist that glimmered like jewels when they caught a streak of sunlight.

Above each type of plant or petal or pod were paintings on the walls that showed them growing in their natural state, with their leaves and berries and roots. And attached to every bundle or basket or flagon were labels with hieroglyphic inscriptions such as SCENTED GIU GRASS FROM THE OASES, ROOTS OF THE BEARDED IRIS, AROMATIC NUBIAN RUSH, SEF WAN OIL FROM THE WOOD OF THE SYRIAN JUNIPER, ROOT OF INDIAN SPIKENARD, CROCUS STAMENS FOR KHYPRI, OIL OF MEREH NAR KERNELS, and many others.

The words seemed like some strange, foreign language.

"Come here!" Intef commanded. "Close your

eyes and hold a piece of this bark, one in each hand, and tell me the difference."

He handed each of us two finger-length quills of bark that looked almost identical.

"They're both cinnamon bark," I said.

Intef shook his head. "Don't make snap decisions. Smell them."

I glanced at Isikara. Her eyes were still closed, and she was breathing evenly and deeply, sniffing each quill in turn. "My left hand holds cinnamon, but the one in my right hand is different. Hotter. More pungent. Almost rose-smelling. It's not cinnamon. It's cassia bark."

"What?" The old man turned his head sharply, but his eyes were milky as usual. "How did you know that? Have you worked with unguents before?"

Isikara nodded. "My father was the embalmer Henuka."

"Henuka? The high priest at the Temple of Sobek? I knew him well. We exchanged methods and recipes."

Isikara looked puzzled. "I've never met you before."

"Of course you wouldn't have met me." He

sounded vexed. "I've lived in the unguent rooms all my life. As holder of the recipes of secret perfumes, I've never been allowed farther than this courtyard."

"Never been farther than this courtyard?"

Intef shook his head. "I corresponded with your father secretly through a scribe. We had the same beliefs. If you've learned at your father's side, you'll be a good alchemist. But your friend from Naharin will have to work in the flower-pressing room. She has no flare for odors."

"How do you know I won't learn?" I snapped. "And how do you know I'm from Naharin?"

"The answer to both questions is, I hear by your voice. When you're blind, your ears tell what your eyes cannot see."

"But that was *bark*. I know grasses and flowers. I've sat in fields of flowers that are so vibrant they burn the eyes. . . ." I bit my lip, realizing the stupidity of mentioning colors.

Isikara interrupted. "I can't stay here. I returned to Thebes to take over my father's position at the Temple of Sobek."

Intef shrugged. "The god Sobek has fallen out of

favor. Besides, the highest of high priests has other plans for you!"

"Wosret? What are his plans?"

The old man waved his arms about as if trying to waft odors and perfumes around to present them to a client. "It's not for me to say."

20

THE PALACE STABLES

Nefertiti rose early. The morning mist hung low over the river. She dressed in a plain linen robe and arranged her wig with the help of her favorite serving girl, Sitra. Then she slipped out of her quarters.

The garden in her courtyard was bathed in cool green light, but already she could see the quivering heat haze rising from the stone paving. The day was going to be scorching hot. With a wave of her hand she bade Sitra stand aside.

"Don't follow me, Sitra. I want to be alone to think."

Then she set out alone to accomplish her plan.

The time for standing alongside Amenhotep in his chariot was gone. She would drive her *own* horses and her *own* chariot to the Temple of Amun. Her chariot was newly built and painted and gilded and stood ready waiting. Now was the time. Tomorrow she would ride out and greet the sun while it poured forth its golden light and the waters of the Great River shimmered back.

She would show Thebes she was worthy of admiration and adoration. At the unveiling of the new Royal Temple of Gempaaten, she would step from the royal barge and lead the procession up through the sphinx-lined avenue to the great gateposts of the Temple of Amun, for all to see that she was queen not only of Egypt but queen of the gods.

She walked around the lake and beyond the formal gardens, until she came to the stables, with their raw smell of oats and straw and horses. She had chosen her own pair of horses. A pair of matching chestnut stallions that the old Naharin horse handler had said were not too frisky but were fiery and powerful enough to be worthy of her.

There was a movement at the far end of the stalls. A stable boy was brushing down a horse. She approached quietly and watched as his hands worked expertly over the milk white flank of the animal.

"You do that well. That's one of Amenhotep's new Assyrian horses."

He dropped the brush and stood up quickly.

"There's no need to stop."

He was older than she'd at first thought.

He looked directly at her with his shoulders thrown back. "You're too early if you are looking for any of the horse handlers or the stable vizier. There's no one here."

"You're here."

He twitched his shoulders impatiently.

"But don't let me stop you from your work. I've come to see my horses."

"*Your* horses?" he snorted. "These horses here belong to the new king."

She narrowed her eyes, and then laughed. "*And* the new queen! Don't forget she owns them as well."

"Yes, she has two stallions. But they're for show.

She's fond of putting on a show. I've never seen her with them. I don't think she knows a thing about horses. She isn't the type. She doesn't care much for horses, if you ask me."

"I didn't ask you, but since you've told me, *I've* seen her with them. They're chestnut stallions."

"Have you now?" He took a step closer and put his hand on her arm. "Well, then, you keep a closer watch on the queen than I. I've never seen her here at the stables. If you know so much, you must be one of her maids. But if you're a maid, and a very pretty maid at that, why would you be here talking about horses and flirting with me? Why wouldn't you be in her quarters attending to her demands?"

"A *maid*? And *flirting*? With *you!*" She flashed her eyes at him. And then checked herself. Yes. Why not? Why shouldn't she play a little teasing game? He was handsome, after all. She smiled. "Judging by the height of the sun, the queen's probably still fast asleep in her quarters."

"They say she's very demanding and spoiled."

Nefertiti's mouth twitched. "Maybe."

"And she likes giving orders."

"Perhaps."

He stopped brushing and gave her a quick look. "You're not going to repeat all this to her, are you?"

She tried to hide her smile and shook her head. "There'd be no need."

"No need?" A sudden look of surprise crossed his face. He stood upright and stared back at her. "What do you mean . . . no need?" Then he took a quick step backward. "You're not? You can't be!"

She stood laughing at him and nodded.

"Don't fool with me! You're setting out to tease!" He reached out and took hold of her shoulders and turned her around to face the sunlight. "I'd know if—" Then his hands sprang away from her shoulders, as if burned by the touch of her skin. They fell helplessly to his sides. "By my breath, I'm done for! That perfume! I should have recognized that perfume. You wore it on the royal barge that day on the river. It floated back to me afterward. Lilies and bergamot and fragrances that words can't even begin to describe. And now here you are! *Queen Nefertiti!* In real life!"

He looked about hurriedly as if sure someone would come and strike him down. He fell to the straw at her feet. "I'm done for! Forgive me!"

She tipped the toe of her sandal at his shoulder.

"Get up, stupid boy! You don't have to do that. I could have you whipped. But I knew you hadn't guessed my secret. I was playing a game. I wanted to see how long it would take you to guess."

"But why? And where are your attendants?" He stood up and turned away abruptly. "I'll be in serious trouble for talking to you."

"Wait!" She took hold of his arm. "Don't dare turn away from me! You'll be in serious trouble for *not* talking to me! Where are my horses?"

"Over there in the stables."

"Over there in the stables, my *queen*, is what you're supposed to say! Take me to them, then."

"It's better if you wait for the stable vizier."

She raised her eyebrows. "'*My queen!*'"

He bowed. "It's better if you wait for the stable vizier, my queen."

She flicked with the tip of her sandal at a piece of straw that had stuck to his leather boot. "You forget. I'm Queen Nefertiti. I'm demanding and spoiled, remember. I'm used to giving orders. And I wait for no one. I want to see them *now*. What's your name?"

He shook his head. "There's no need of a name."

"'My *queen!*'" she insisted, then shrugged. "Well, I'm ordering you . . ." She couldn't stop a smile from creeping across her face. This boy was handsome. She was pleased she'd worn a simple robe. Its pleats hung well. She knew it suited her. "No, perhaps I'm *asking* you to take me to my horses."

A faint smile seemed to curl around the corners of his lips then. He lifted an eyebrow. "What about your thin sandals and the edges of your robe? You're not dressed for entering a stable."

She tossed her head. "No matter. I want to discuss how the horses must look when they draw my chariot to the Temple of Amun tomorrow."

"Who will be your driver?"

"I'll be my *own* driver." She bent down to stroke a cat that was rubbing itself against her legs.

"That's unheard of for a queen."

She looked up from the cat. "I plan a lot that's unheard of."

He smiled broadly for the first time. "You've a keen eye for a horse. You've chosen your pair of stallions well."

"I thought you said the queen knew *nothing* about horses!" she teased.

He bowed. "I'm suitably rebuked on all counts."

Then he stood back to allow her to enter the stable, and pointed to two stalls beside each other. "They're tethered, but be careful. They're powerful horses and could harm you if they reared."

Nefertiti laughed as she touched the arched swan neck of the closest horse. "I like their rich color. I think leopard skin headgear with plumes of ostrich and a red tasseled cloak is needed for each horse. What do you think?"

He lounged up against the door frame and smiled. "It's not for me to think but to obey!"

She gave him a sidelong look. Now who was teasing whom? For a stable hand he certainly had swagger. He would be a handsome chariot runner to have at her side. She could show him off in front of the ladies on the way to the temple.

Her eyes flashed in the dim light of the stables. "I want you as my chariot runner tomorrow. One of my pet cheetahs will run alongside you. I dare you to accept!"

They both turned at the noise of someone entering the courtyard.

"Quick, decide!" Then she looked directly at him again. "I could order your obedience, you know!"

He gave a curt bow, then turned and hastily disappeared out a side door.

At the same moment the main entrance to the stables was blocked by the frame of a large man.

"Your Majesty!" The stable vizier drew a sharp breath and tugged clumsily at his tunic to check it was properly tied before he bowed. "This is unexpected. If I'd known you'd planned to visit us so early, I'd have been here to receive you, my queen." He waved his arms about as if swatting at gnats. "Where are your attendants? And won't your sandals be ruined?"

She shrugged. "Sandals are easily replaced. I came to check whether my horses and chariot will be ready for tomorrow."

"But you could've sent a messenger. And, ready? Ready for *what*, my queen?"

"I'll be driving my chariot tomorrow to the unveiling of the new Royal Temple of Gempaaten."

"But I wasn't told."

"You're told now! See that it is ready."

He bowed. "Everything has been done to your orders. The chariot has been gilded and painted with your cartouche. The wheels are of the latest design, six-spoked, each spoke light and well shaped. The carriage is woven for delicacy and lightness so the horses will appear as if they are carrying no more than a feather." He bowed. "Which indeed is the case, my queen. But . . ."

"But what?"

"I cannot . . . ," he blundered.

"'Cannot allow'? Is that what you were going to say?"

"Your Majesty, should you do this? Is it safe?"

"Of course it is! I hope you've made sure the chariot doesn't squeak. I can't abide creaking chariots that screech at every wheel turn. It truly vexes me. Amenhotep's chariot was creaking yesterday like an old man's bones. It turns a chariot ride into a silly debacle. I expected people to start laughing at any moment."

"I'm sorry you were vexed, my queen. We've lined your chariot's hubs and axle with copper plates so there'll be no screech of wood against wood, and the wheels have rawhide lashed to them to make them more silent."

"Well, make sure the lashing doesn't wear away. I don't want the sound of flapping rawhide following me along the way!"

He bowed. "The lashing is set in grooves to

prevent any wear. It won't break. And the harnesses for the horses are made of dyed calfskin and have been studded with silver. The horses will be wearing ivory blinkers."

"Good! I've instructed your stable boy that I want them dressed with ostrich plumes and red tasseled cloaks as well."

The vizier looked puzzled. "My stable boy? No stable boy has arrived yet."

She waved her hand. "Well, I spoke to someone. He'll tell you what I want. He was here a moment ago. And I want him as my chariot runner beside me."

Nefertiti gathered her robe to prevent it from dragging in the straw as she stepped past.

"But—"

"Make certain it's done, and make sure my chariot doesn't squeak!"

21

SECRETS OF THE UNGUENT ROOMS

We were put to work by Intef. I was sent to the flower-pressing room and Isikara to the main unguent room, where she worked at a bench blending oils and grinding resins and weighing powders on a balance, like Thoth making judgments.

We hardly saw each other, and at night we were so tired we fell asleep without speaking. Intef was strict with us. When the rose petals were delivered to the courtyard by the gardeners early each morning, we weren't allowed to waste time gossiping. I eyed the men and tried to choose one who might bring me word of Samut.

The other girls kept up a list of instructions. "Spread them on the tables under the reed awnings before they bruise. Leave them long enough for the sun to dry the dew. But not long enough for the petals to go limp. Then they must be steeped overnight."

"Do you ever get the chance to talk to the gardeners?" I whispered.

They shook their heads.

"Never?" My heart sank.

The girl next to me smiled and whispered. "We don't have to *talk*! We use sign language. That way Intef doesn't know we're gossiping or flirting with one another!"

"I'm trying to find news of a boy called Samut."

She laughed. "Samut? You don't have to ask the *gardeners*. We know Samut well."

I looked around at the group of them as their hands flew over the petals. "'*We*'? Do *all* of you know him?"

She nodded. "There's probably not one girl in this courtyard who he hasn't kissed."

I stared around. "He's kissed *all* of you?"

The girl next to me shrugged. "What's a kiss from a boy as handsome as Samut?" Then she stopped briefly and searched my face. "What do you want with him? You're not in *love* with him, are you? He's not worthy of true love."

"Stop this chatter and get off to the pressing room," Intef growled. "There are petals that have been steeping overnight and are waiting to be squeezed out. And mind you, rub out the collecting vessels with honey first and rub your hands properly with honey too before you toss today's petals in the oil. Be sure to follow the recipe exactly. Get along with you now."

The girls moved quickly to the press room. The recipe for rose oil was painted on one of the mud walls.

- 2 baskets of camel grass bruised and macerated.
- Boiled up with 9 jugs of green olive oil.
- 1,000 rose petals steeped in the above.
- Honey for coating the hands and vessels.
- Salt as a fixative to prevent spoilage.
- Alkanet roots to make a red dye tincture.

There were other recipes on the walls as well. One for lily oil, and one called the Royal that had so many ingredients, the list went right down to the floor. It was as if every aroma gathered from every part of the world was in it.

But it was rose oil we were making today.

I couldn't concentrate as the girls gathered large linen bags. They lifted the steeping jars from the day before and poured the petals and oil through the linen bags into a huge jar smeared with honey. Then they twisted a stick into each corner of a bag and showed me how to squeeze out the last drop of essence from the mixture.

"Twist as hard you can. Twist as if you are wringing out washing."

I twisted until I thought my wrists would break. I twisted as if it were Samut's neck. How could he have kissed them all?

A girl at my side gave me a look. "Your hands will get used to it. Calluses will form where you once had blisters. You're the Naharin girl, aren't you? The one they arrested for stealing a ring?"

"I didn't steal it."

"No matter. We know who stole it."

"It wasn't stolen. It was a copy of the real ring."

"A copy?" She gave me a look. "He really *has* fooled you."

"Who?"

"Samut, of course! We all know he's a tomb robber."

I looked at her sharply. "*How* do you know?"

"He has charmed us all with his trinkets." She nodded her head toward a girl twisting a stick. "See that charm around her neck?"

My voice hardly dared to whisper, "From Samut?"

She nodded and whispered hurriedly, "Make yourself busy. Here comes Intef." Then she spoke louder for his benefit. "This is the first oil. But the same rose petals get steeped in fresh oil again and are squeezed again for the second oil."

Intef nodded. "Four times with the same petals. Then the oil is dyed with alkanet because its color reflects the redness of the rose. Color and clarity are as important as smell."

I looked at him.

"Yes, I know what you're thinking. How will I know? I can *smell* murkiness! So watch out for sloppy work. No one wants a murky perfume the color of mud. Least of all Nefertiti!"

I looked down at the blisters that were beginning to form on my hands. All for the benefit of Nefertiti! A pestilence of flies on her!

When Intef left, the girl nudged me. "Your friend, that girl working on the bench in the unguent room, had better be careful."

"Careful? Why?"

"Haven't you noticed?"

"What?"

"All the workers alongside her are blind."

"Are you sure?"

"Of course I'm sure! Only blind people are employed on the bench. They've a better sense of smell because they aren't distracted. We call them sniffers."

"What's this to do with Isikara?"

"If you're good, they blind you to improve your sense of smell."

"What? I don't believe you!"

She shrugged. "You haven't worked here long enough!"

"But surely they're employed in the unguent rooms because they're already blind? Because they're *born* blind, like Intef?"

She nodded. "Some. But not *all*!"

That night as we lay on our pallets in the workers' quarters, I felt I had to warn Isikara. "You have to pretend to be hopeless."

"In the name of Horus, why? I enjoy doing what I do. Why should I pretend I'm hopeless?"

I told her what the girl had said.

"Did you ask her to swear by Maat's feather?" she whispered.

I shook my head. "I forgot."

"Well, then, it *can't* be true. Intef would *never* agree to have me blinded. He knew my father. And besides, Tuthmosis wouldn't allow it."

"So where is Tuthmosis? He hasn't come to rescue you."

"Nor has your friend," she whispered back at me. "Tuthmosis has to speak to his brother first."

"That'll be no help if you're already blinded."

"They're *not* going to blind me."

"How can you be sure?"

"Intef has discovered I can read. He's chosen scrolls for me to study. They are written up by the scribe who follows him around making notes. They're kept in sealed boxes in the Chamber of Secrets below the unguent rooms. *The Book of Heavenly Oils,*

The Book of Unguents for Unsealing the Heart, and *The Book of Moon Secrets.* The fragrances are all made according to the moon cycles. The recipes are written in hieratic script and are easy to follow even though some words are strange and foreign. Why would he blind me? If I were blinded, I wouldn't be able to read them back to him."

"*Exactly!* He's given you the scrolls to read so you can memorize the recipes and ingredients *before* you're blinded."

"Intef wouldn't do that!"

"How can you be sure?"

"I've discovered his secret. He needs me."

"What's his secret?"

"He's anosmic."

"Anosmic? What's that?"

"He's lost his sense of smell."

"*What?* I don't believe you!"

"Shhh! Keep your voice low. It's true. I've been watching the way he works. He simply carries on from memory, creating perfumes that he presents with great gravity, pretending to sniff as he waves the odor around the room. But he no longer knows for sure. He can't smell *anything.*"

"But how can you be a perfume maker if you can't see *and* you can't smell?"

"Precisely! I'm the only one who's guessed his secret. The others can't see how puzzled his face is sometimes. He needs me as his eyes *and* his nose. He knows his secret is safe with me because of his friendship with my father."

"You can't rely on it!" Suddenly a thought struck me. "And it won't only be *you* they'll blind. You said yourself. Nefertiti has accused us *both* of helping Tuthmosis."

Isikara pulled her sleeping pallet closer to mine. "Don't fret, Ta-Miu. Nefertiti won't order it. We'll escape soon. I'll think of something. What's gotten into you? Why're you so jumpy?"

"The girls are full of stories."

"About what?"

"About . . ." Without planning to, I found I was telling her about Samut. At first I didn't say his name.

But then finally I did say it.

All the time, I kept wishing I could stop.

But I couldn't.

All the time, I kept thinking she would say, *You deserved this! You told a secret you shouldn't have told.*

But she didn't.

All the time, I thought she would interrupt and say he was a rogue and not worth defending. That I should speak out against him.

But she kept silent and listened while I talked and talked.

Eventually I blurted out, "The flower room girls say Samut has kissed them *all*."

In the darkness I heard Isikara begin to laugh. "So *that's* what's gotten into you! You're jealous!"

22

GEMPAATEN, HOUSE OF THE SUN DISK

The hot, sultry night brought little sleep to Nefertiti. Not even the slightest breeze wafted up from the river as she tossed about on her bed.

She turned this way and that while thought followed thought as fast as falcons after prey, and idea sparked idea and plan was added to plan. Her decision was the right one. Today she would begin its execution. Whatever might happen, she was prepared.

Wosret had had the girl Isikara arrested for helping Tuthmosis escape. But now Nefertiti had heard that both Isikara and Tadukhepa's maid had been taken from prison and moved to the palace perfumery.

The order could only have come from Amenhotep.

As soon as the stars faded, she called her chief attendant. "Sitra, listen carefully. Today when we celebrate the new Gempaaten Temple, be sure everyone is ready. The fan bearers, the cheetah handlers, my grooms and chariot runners. Nothing must go wrong. They must all be in their places."

"It's all arranged, my lady, as we discussed yesterday."

"See that the gold menat necklaces for handing out are ready and the bouquets for the offerings are fresh. I want red poppies and bright blue cornflowers so they show against my robe. And see that the women who play the sistrums have checked their instruments. I can't stand rusty rattles that have no tune to them."

"I ordered new copper sistrums to be made. They've been coated with a mixture of silver and gold so they'll catch the sunlight and reflect the glory of Aten. Each and every disk has been checked to see that it runs freely on the wires," Sitra replied.

Nefertiti smiled. "You've thought of everything, Sitra. I'll need two crowns. The Khepresh warrior crown exactly the same as my husband's, except mine must have red streamers, for when I drive my chariot. And the double Atef crown with the tall plumes and sun disk for the ceremony inside our new temple to the sun. See that the plumes are identical in height to those on my husband's crown."

"Both are ready on their stands. I've chosen a bombyx silk for you to wear, as fine and transparent as cobweb. Don't be nervous, my lady. Everything will go smoothly."

"Nervous? I'm not nervous, Sitra. Today must be perfect. Everyone must know I'm the Queen of Two Lands. Mistress of Egypt."

"They will love you. The crowds are *already* gathering. They have lined the palace road all the way to the banks of the river and are gathered on the other side as well. A queen has never been so adored in Egypt."

Nefertiti picked up her bronze hand mirror, with its circle of amethysts, and checked her reflection. Was her stomach just beginning to show?

"Is there any more news of Tuthmosis? What's the palace gossip, Sitra?"

"Don't worry. He can't take the throne from you. The people of Thebes would *never* allow it. Especially now that you will give birth to the future king."

"Pray to Hathor it's a boy. But *why* has he returned, Sitra? Why didn't he stay in Nubia?"

"Don't fret, my lady." She rested her hands firmly on Nefertiti's shoulders. "You don't want creases on your forehead today. Thebes is waiting."

After the painter of the eyes added the final sweep of galena paste to her eyelids and the painter of the mouth made the final stroke of color on her lips, Nefertiti took one last look in her mirror and then smiled at Sitra.

She was ready to dazzle them all.

Amenhotep was waiting beside the double palanquin reserved for special occasions, wearing the elaborate triple Atef crown flanked by rising cobras and topped with falcons bearing a sun disk and a double cartouche. A leopard cloak was slung over his shoulder, with the head and paws of the animal hanging heavily across his chest, and the eyes set with two magnificent sparkling emeralds. The clasp holding the skin, the gold belt circling his waist, the wide armbands above his elbows, and the pectoral collar on his chest all glittered and flashed with gems.

Nefertiti caught his eye and smiled as they bowed formally to each other. He looked exceedingly handsome and much older than his fifteen years. For a moment she forgot that she was cross with him for freeing Isikara and Ta-Miu from prison.

The king and queen were helped into the golden double palanquin with its lion figures and striking cobras. It took fifteen men to lift it from the ground. Nefertiti wrapped her arm around Amenhotep's waist to steady herself while the bearers hoisted the poles up on their shoulders. Led by fan bearers and priests swinging purifying censers, the palanquin was carried across a second courtyard toward the great double cedar doors of the Inner Palace. Servants, attendants, and bodyguards carrying bows and shields, and wearing feathers to mark the celebration, stood waiting to join the retinue.

As Nefertiti heard the clamor of the crowds outside the palace, a shiver of anticipation ran through her. Then the great outer gates were flung open wide and a roar of delight greeted her.

She smiled and took Amenhotep's hand as he

helped her from the palanquin. "We have to speak," she said under her breath as she turned to wave at the cheering crowd.

Amenhotep nodded and smiled in all directions. "What's so urgent that it cannot wait until after the ceremony?"

"You've allowed the two girl prisoners to go free."

"They're not free. They're working locked up in the unguent rooms. We can discuss this later."

The chariots for the procession stood lined up and gleaming in the sunshine. In front of them pairs of horses stamped and chafed at being held back by their handlers.

Nefertiti's chariot was not in the lead as she had ordered but stood behind Amenhotep's.

She turned to some serving girls and exchanged her tall-plumed crown for the warrior crown.

She looked at Amenhotep. "I suggest you wear yours as well." Then she strode toward her chariot without waiting for him. A groom helped her mount the small step at the back. She took up the reins and edged the horses forward so that the chariot stood in line with the king's.

A smile crept across her face as she looked at

Amenhotep. "Let's have some fun. Let's have a race! Just you and I."

Without waiting, amidst cheering and drum-beats and dust, she cracked her whip. Her chestnut horses sprang forward. Her horse handler sprinted beside her. Her chariot runner dashed ahead leading a cheetah—not the handsome boy, unfortunately. She wished she'd *commanded* the stable boy to be her runner. He would've added a final flourish to the scene.

Officials and bodyguards, taken by surprise, tried to keep back the throng of people in her pathway.

"My lady, my lady! Slow down!" her horse handler shouted as he gasped for breath alongside the flying hooves.

The horses gathered speed. Nefertiti sensed the ribbons on her warrior crown and the silk of her robe streaming out behind her. She sensed too the appreciation of the crowd as they clapped and cheered and urged her on. With the hot wind against her face, she glanced sideways to see Amenhotep gaining on her.

Then she cracked her whip and clung to the rail of her chariot, laughing as the horses galloped all the faster through the passageway between the people.

For now she had made her point.

Her plans were coming together.

All of Thebes loved her. Now the next step was to deal with the two girls.

Nefertiti and Amenhotep drew up breathlessly at the quayside to board the royal barge, which would take them across the Great River and up the newly dug canal, right to the quayside of the Temple of Amun.

As her feet touched the ground, she glanced playfully back at Amenhotep. "Did you enjoy that?" Her breath was coming in gasps.

"Should a queen do that? Do you think it was wise?"

"Wise? How can a race be wise?" She laughed and then shrugged. "Who wants to be wise when you can have fun?"

"You might have fallen and hurt yourself. And now especially . . ." But his voice trailed off in confusion.

Nefertiti touched his cheek. "Don't worry. The baby is safe." She straightened his warrior crown. "You're *so* handsome today in your cloak and finery." Then she turned and stepped on board the *Dazzling Aten.*

Her attendants changed her warrior crown for the double-feathered Atef crown and rearranged her robe, in time for her to take up position under the red canopy of the royal barge at Amenhotep's side.

As the king and queen sailed along the Temple of Amun's quay, they were greeted by an even larger and more boisterous crowd. The chariots and horses had been ferried across and were waiting on the other side to carry them along the avenue of sphinx-headed rams that led from the river to the temple. The air was thick with the perfume of sacred oils already sprinkled on the paving.

Now the pace of the chariots was slow and leisurely while women rattling sistrums went before them and priests purified the air ahead with swinging censers.

Nefertiti smiled and waved as the crowds craned their necks to see through the clouds of swirling incense smoke and reached out to try to touch the spoke of a wheel or the tassel of a tunic as the king and queen passed.

At the entrance to the Great Hall, with its high ceiling and gigantic columns, the chariots halted. Wosret came forward in his priestly leopard cloak and greeted them with a bow.

"I heard the crowd. It seems you've tamed the whole of Thebes," he whispered to Nefertiti. Then he nodded at Amenhotep. "Shall we proceed?"

He led them forward through the dark hall lit by flares that accentuated the great height of the columns and the ceiling far above their heads.

As they came to the gate built by Amenhotep's father, Nefertiti drew up sharply. Her eyes swept over the words that told of her father-in-law's greatness.

I, Amenhotep,

king of Upper and Lower Egypt, ruler

of Thebes, have built this monument

to Amun and have made

a great bark of new cedar,

which was dragged over the mountains

by the princes of all countries.

There is none like it.

Its hull is adorned with gold

and its shrine coated with silver

so that it fills the land with its brightness.

Nefertiti cast a moody eye across the carving of the barge below, which showed the old king holding the steering oar, while a human-headed sphinx with a cheetah's body perched in the prow of the bark above a wedjat eye.

"These inscriptions and carvings must be changed to include mine and my husband's names!"

Wosret sighed. "All in good time! All in good time, Nefertiti! Today we celebrate your new temple complex, Gempaaten, where there are plenty of inscriptions to you. But first we must make offerings to Amun."

They came to the bolted entrance of the great cedar door that led to the innermost sanctuary of the Temple of Amun. Wosret cleansed the air with burning incense. Then he asked Amenhotep to break the clay seal on the lion-shaped bolt that barred the door. This was the holiest of holy places, where no other person could enter except the king and queen and he, Wosret, the highest of high priests.

It was built of sandstone from the red mountain and was lined with a mix of shining gold and silver. In it stood the statue of Amun alongside a lyre made of silver, gold, lapis lazuli, and green malachite. Amenhotep held up his hawk-headed censing spoon, filled with burning spices of myrrh and khypri, and made offerings. Then Nefertiti stepped forward and laid down the huge bouquet of red poppies, cornflowers, lilies, and lotus flowers on the offering table and made her incantation.

Wosret led them out into a courtyard on the eastern side and along a walkway to the Royal Temple of Gempaaten. It had been built by the order of the new king, Amenhotep the Younger, to worship the sun itself. It faced east to catch the first of Aten's rays. It was so newly built that grains of sand still crunched on the paving under their sandals, its halls smelled of newly hewn stone, and the gardeners had barely had time to transform the mudflats around it into a place of greenery.

Amenhotep, Nefertiti, and Wosret took up their places on the Balcony of Appearances. Nefertiti rested her elbows on the squashy red bolsters that lined the parapet, and she looked down on the crowds that were pushing forward into the courtyard below. A deafening din of shouts of welcome, greetings, shrieks of delight, applause, and cheering rose up and almost drowned the sounds of the flutes, tambourines, lutes, lyres, and a harp so large it was played by two musicians, one on either side of it.

Nefertiti took the gold crescent-shaped menat

necklaces encrusted with jewels that Sitra and the other attendants were holding. She stood in profile so that people would notice the bump of her stomach. Then she held each menat necklace high so that it glittered and sparkled in the sunlight like a crescent sun. And with a smile just as dazzling, she tossed each one down separately into the crowd and watched while people clamored and grabbed and blessed her for her kindness.

Out of the corner of her eye she caught sight of the other wives standing and watching. Among them was the pretty little princess from Naharin. Now was the time to strike. Amenhotep would not be able to refuse. He smiled and waved alongside her, mesmerized by the excitement of the people below.

"Listen to me, Amenhotep. They must be blinded!" Nefertiti said.

He turned distractedly. "Blinded? Who? These people? What do you mean?"

"The two girls."

"What?" He stared back at her. "Who are you talking of, Nefertiti?"

"The girls, Isikara and the maid from Naharin, must be blinded!"

"Why?"

"True perfume makers can be sure of their sense of smell only if not distracted by other senses. The best perfume makers are always blind. Your mother always said this!"

Amenhotep shook his head. Over the roar of the crowd, his voice was harsh. "Yes, but born blind. You have enough blind perfume makers. And Intef is the best in the world. You're going too far."

She smiled back at him. "*I'm* not to blame that the two girls were made perfume makers. It was *you* who put them to work in the unguent rooms in the first place."

23

THE FEATHER OF MAAT

The gardeners who delivered the rose petals wouldn't meet my eye. I kept glancing at them as they off-loaded their baskets, thinking they might have news of Samut. But no one would return my look. Even the girls from the flower-pressing room slid their glances past me and started whispering with their heads bent low as they spread the petals on the drying tables, so I couldn't catch a word of what they said.

One of them looked up at me. I thought she was about to speak, but Intef came by, and she busied herself again.

I felt a prickle run through me. What were they hiding?

Then, before we'd even strained the jars from the previous day's steeping, I heard the sound of raised voices in the courtyard. My body turned to stone.

What if Nefertiti had decided? What if we were both being fetched right now?

A man strode into the room and grabbed my arms. I shrugged him off. "Let go of me!"

The room was completely silent now, with not a sound from the girls as they watched.

I stood with my back against the wall.

"What? What have I done? Why're you all so silent? Say something!" I stared around at the girls' faces. Those who met my eyes looked terrified, then looked quickly away again.

The man jerked my arms behind my back. "Don't delay! I'm under orders to fetch you."

Across the room my eyes met the eyes of the girl who'd first warned me. She'd said it would be Isikara. She'd said nothing of me.

I was brought from the darkness into the bright sunshine of the courtyard. *Concentrate,* I kept urging myself. *This is the last day you'll see sunlight and rose petals in shades from darkest red to delicate orange and palest pink. Print the colors on your mind forever. Soak up everything like the desert soaks up dew. And pray to Hathor that you'll never let them be lost from your head. From now onward there will always be darkness.*

My head was spinning. Despite the heat, I began to shake. I saw across the courtyard that they were holding Isikara. Then I saw Kiya standing there too.

Why was she here?

"Stay away, Kiya," I shouted. But the guard pushed me forward. I beat against his chest and stumbled, so that Kiya reached out a hand to steady me.

"Don't worry," she whispered. "They won't hurt you. You have to speak out."

What? What was she saying?

"Just tell the truth," she whispered. "Save yourself. Tell that Samut gave you the ring and not Tuthmosis."

"Tell *who?*"

"Amenhotep. I've pleaded with him. If you admit it was Samut, neither you nor Isikara will be blinded. He has promised."

"Isikara has nothing to do with Samut!"

"Wosret has convinced Nefertiti you were both involved in the tomb robbing. And you both helped Tuthmosis escape. So you must both be punished. All you have to do is speak the truth."

I felt the blood drain from my face. Then it came seething back again. My skin seemed to pulse with heat. I swallowed and tried to protest. But no words came. Surely Kiya would know it was impossible. I couldn't speak out against Samut.

Yet if I stayed silent, Isikara would be blinded as well.

Nefertiti had given me two choices: speak or lose my sight. I couldn't bear either.

I needed the strength of the seventeenth lion to roar in the queen's face.

Across the courtyard Isikara was watching me. Who would they take first? A shudder ran through me. Too late. The guards forced us both toward the gate. My feet slid over the gravel and my legs went lame.

Kiya nodded curtly at the guards. "Release them both! They're in my care now. I'll take them to the Great Hall."

The guard scowled at her. "We were told to accompany you."

"Well, accompany us, then, but don't hold them so brutally. They're not trussed goats being led to slaughter, but women."

"Prisoners, no less!"

"They won't be prisoners after the king has heard what they have to say."

I glanced at her. This was a new Kiya.

A sneer swept over the guard's face. "How can you be so sure?"

"Do as I say. Release them!"

Isikara turned. "Wait! There is something I must fetch." She was gone only for a few moments, and then we were on our way, with the guards begrudgingly following at a distance.

I looked at Kiya and forced myself to speak. "Are we truly to be blinded?"

She glanced at me. "Only if you remain silent, Ta-Miu! Be brave now. Remember on our journey from Mitanni to Egypt when I was scared, you kept telling me 'Don't fear tomorrow while today's sun is still in the sky.'"

But as we got to the huge cedar doors that were

swung open by attendants, I felt myself falter. Not only Amenhotep but also Nefertiti sat waiting on the golden thrones, wearing the tall red crown of Upper Egypt. Nefertiti's cheetahs prowled restlessly around the room, their tails swinging heavily and their nails *tick-tick*ing against the tiles. And standing beside their thrones, swathed in his snarling leopard skin cloak, was Wosret.

Isikara gasped. She gripped my hand. When I turned to her, I could see the fear in her eyes. "May Sekhmet protect us! If Wosret's to decide our fate, I'm done for!" she whispered.

I looked back at her. "It's not Wosret. It's *me* who has to decide!"

Kiya urged me forward. "Speak the truth now, Ta-Miu. Tell them it was *Samut* who broke into the tomb."

Samut? My breath caught at the sound of his name. But Isikara couldn't be blinded because of me. Samut had betrayed me. He hadn't come for me. My decision was made. I nodded. "I'll speak."

Amenhotep held up his hand. "Wait." He beckoned to a scribe to start recording the proceedings and for an attendant to step forward. The attendant held out a long white ostrich plume. "Lay your hand on the feather of Maat. Swear you speak the truth."

I bowed and touched the plume. My fingers were shaking so much they made the fronds of the feather shiver. "By the feather of Maat, I do."

"All you say will be recorded and upheld as the truth on this matter from now onward."

I bowed.

"Then, proceed."

I felt Kiya and Isikara stand close on either side of me.

I began the story of how I'd first met Samut. How I'd told him about the duplicate ankh key that opened the lock on the gate of the secret passageway that led into the great king Amenhotep's burial chamber.

The words caught in my throat, but eventually my voice got stronger and stronger. As my story grew, I sensed the quietness in the Great Hall as they listened, as silent as mice before the stare of a cat.

And so I damned Samut. And damned myself.

There was only the sound of my voice, hoarse now, as I spoke the last words, "Isikara should not be blinded! She has suffered more than is needed. Tell your story, Isikara. Tell of why Tuthmosis went to Nubia and who you were fleeing from. And what happened in the war between Egypt and Nubia. Tell of how you came to lose your bow fingers."

Wosret took a sudden step forward. His hand sliced through the air. "Enough! Enough storytelling and rambling." His face was flushed as he glared at Isikara, daring her to defy him. "There's no need for *trivial* confessions."

He bowed toward Nefertiti and Amenhotep. "We don't need further explanations. I recommend a pardon. Let them both be freed. The maid has accused someone by the name of Samut. That's enough evidence. He must be found and punished. There's no need for further unraveling. We need quick action. The thief must be brought to trial immediately."

Isikara tossed her head. Her eyes glinted dangerously as she edged her way past Wosret. She bowed before Amenhotep. "There *is* need for further unraveling. Ta-Miu's story is not the whole story. You've not heard *my* side."

"I said, *enough!* Be silent, girl! You were not asked to speak!" Wosret glowered at Isikara as if he wished his glance would pierce her heart. "There's no need to muddle this with untrue stories."

Amenhotep held up his hand. "Wait, Wosret. This girl speaks with conviction. She's the daughter of Henuka, who was the priest at the Temple of Sobek. Would the daughter of a priest lie?"

Wosret gave Amenhotep a sharp look. Then changed his voice to a tone that was like honey dripping over cake. "You can't believe a girl who has lived a rough life among men in army camps. She's hardly the sort of person you can trust to speak the truth. Her brother is a mercenary. He's paid by the Nubians to fight *against* Egypt. In the desert she became friends with a girl who murdered a Medjay leader. She and Tuthmosis took up arms against Egypt. She's not just a liar but a *traitor.*"

Isikara swung to face him so suddenly that one of the cheetahs snarled at her. "The girl didn't murder the man. *I* did. To set her free of him. She was enslaved by him. You paid that same Medjay leader to be your spy. And *you*—"

"Enough!"

Isikara spoke all the louder. "*You* would've paid him to see both Tuthmosis and me killed, but we escaped!"

"What proof have you?"

"This!" Isikara held up a thick bundle of papyrus that she'd grabbed from her girdle bag. "Intef hid this for me in the Chamber of Secrets with his scrolls. It's all written here. I kept a record of everything that happened on our journey to Nubia and back. It begins with the words: 'With two fingers missing, it's hard to grip a reed stylus.' I wrote with difficulty because of Wosret's soldiers. They chopped off my fingers to prevent me from using a bow. But had I not been able to find soot for ink, I'd have written even with my own blood to tell of how Tuthmosis and I were pursued and captured."

Amenhotep stood up. "Is this true, Wosret?"

"*Lies*, my lord! All lies! The desert has done nothing to change this girl's manners. When last we met, she defiled your mother's embalming chamber by *spitting* at me!"

Isikara tossed her head. "I would spit at you again were we not in the Great Hall before the king and queen."

Wosret turned his back abruptly on Isikara. He raised his arms and waved them in front of Amenhotep and Nefertiti as if gathering energy from the air. "You can see for yourselves that the girl is deranged. You can't believe her story! It's all lies. She should be put to death for speaking such treason against *me*, the highest of high priests. Why would I plot to kill the future king of Egypt?"

But Isikara was not to be stopped. "Not only did Wosret try to poison Tuthmosis, but he also killed my father."

Wosret swirled around to face her so quickly that the claws of his leopard cloak snatched at the air. "You have *no* proof I killed your father. He died of grief when he was embalming Queen Tiy. And what possible reason would I have to poison Tuthmosis? I was his trusted mentor."

Amenhotep spoke quietly. "His trust was misplaced."

Wosret glared back at him. "You can't believe this girl's story against mine."

"I wouldn't have. But I received the same account in a message from my brother."

Nefertiti looked startled. "Your *brother*? Tuthmosis has written to you? What did he say? Does he want to take the throne from you?"

"What my brother has written is a private matter. It's clear these girls must go free. I command it."

PART
FOUR

PART
FOUR

24

ACROSS THE RIVER

I 've found the message, my lady." Sitra bowed and took some scraps from her girdle bag. "But the papyrus has been torn to shreds. It's hard to decipher the writing."

Nefertiti reached out. "So you've tried to read it already, Sitra!"

"I wanted to check that it was in fact the letter for your husband."

"Silly Sitra! I'm not chastising you. I'm teasing.

I trust you with my heart. And I'm delighted you found it. Wosret vows he searched everywhere and found no trace of it."

Sitra shook her head. "I think Wosret found it and tore it up. I found it scattered in bits in the rose garden near his quarters. It has Tuthmosis's cartouche on it."

"*Tuthmosis?* Then this is the letter Amenhotep spoke of. So it's true! The message isn't from that little desert fox. Lay it out quickly. Can we put the pieces together and see what Tuthmosis is plotting?" Nefertiti ruffled through the bits of papyrus. "We have to be clever. It's like a puzzle, Sitra."

"Look, my lady. Below Tuthmosis's cartouche, if you take this piece and join it with that one, he asks your husband to meet him."

Nefertiti peered across Sitra's shoulder. "Meet him? Where and why?"

"Here it says 'lake,' and here it says 'night.'"

"Queen Tiy's lake at night? Why would Tuthmosis meet Amenhotep inside the palace grounds if he wants the meeting kept secret? It doesn't make sense. It would be too risky."

Sitra shook her head. "Not Queen Tiy's lake. If

you put this piece next to the other, it makes the words '*sacred* lake.'"

"The Sacred Lake next to the Temple of Amun! Sitra, you deserve five gold menat necklaces as a gift for being such a valuable servant. But it's too risky for Amenhotep to meet with Tuthmosis."

"How so, my lady?"

"Tuthmosis is being too secretive. Why doesn't he come directly to the palace and have a proper meeting with his brother? It can only be that he plans to get Amenhotep to hand over his throne." She gripped the armrests of her chair. "Or . . . maybe he plans to *capture* him."

Sitra's eyebrows shot up. "Shouldn't you speak to Wosret?"

Nefertiti shook her head. "After hearing the accusations against him today, I don't trust him."

Sitra looked alarmed. "Then you must warn Amenhotep not to go."

"Amenhotep loves his brother. He'll never believe me. I won't be able to prevent him from going."

"Then, what *will* you do?"

"Go secretly to the lake at the appointed time."

"How will that help? Rather, suggest to the king that you'll go with him."

"He'll never agree."

"But alone across the river late at night? In your condition? What help would you be?"

"I'll hide and listen and confront Tuthmosis if I'm suspicious."

"You *can't* go alone. Take bodyguards, at least."

"Don't be foolish, Sitra. With an escort of guards I might as well have lyres and drums announce my arrival. No. It has to be secret. You must arrange a boat for me with a boatman who swears to silence. A dagger will be my protection."

"Please don't go alone, I beg you. I'll go with you."

The night was dark and silent. A thick heavy mist over the river muted everything. At the quayside the only sound came from the slap of water against the wooden pylons. Even the frogs were silent.

"A pestilence! Why does it have to be misty tonight of all nights? Can you see anything? Where's the boatman, Sitra? I thought you said you'd arranged everything."

"Don't fret. He'll come. I promised him gold."

Nefertiti searched the darkness. Mist drifted against her face like bits of torn rag. She could barely see across to the other bank. Why couldn't Tuthmosis and Amenhotep have met on the palace side of the river?

Sitra shuddered.

Nefertiti gave her a sharp look. "What's the matter now?"

"I don't like to be so close to the river at night. There could be crocodiles."

"Then, you shouldn't have come. And I wish you hadn't made me wear this scratchy peasant tunic."

"You mustn't be recognized."

"Look!" Nefertiti pointed. "See. Around that bend close to the reeds, there's a shape coming this way. Is it a boat?"

"Praise Horus, let it be!" Sitra let out a sigh.

The dark upturned prow of a boat loomed through the mist. The man rowing it had thrown a cloak around his shoulders and head. He was hardly distinguishable from the shape of the boat itself. There was no flare burning in the prow, but as he came alongside the quay, he held up a small oil lamp. His face remained in shadow under the cloak.

"I was delayed." His voice sounded rough, with a throat used to quaffing strong wine. "There were other boats out on the river. I had to keep to the shadows of the bank."

"No doubt it was Tuthmosis and Amenhotep, both making their separate crossings," Sitra whispered.

"Hurry now. Step into the boat. I can't hold it forever alongside the quay in this current," the boat-man said brusquely, without extending a hand to help Nefertiti. It was clear he had no idea who she was.

Once she and Sitra were in the boat, he edged quickly away from the quay. The Great River ran silently as he dipped his oars into the dark, syrupy surface. Somewhere out in the middle of the river the mist suddenly evaporated. The water turned to silver, with the moonlight catching and shattering against each ripple. A sky heavy with stars opened above them.

In the boat all three were silent. Now they were out in the main stream in full view of anyone who might be watching.

Across on the opposite bank Nefertiti saw the first gateway of the temple looming up. The eastern bank was much darker than she'd expected. Surely there should have been flares burning somewhere to light the way? She'd never been out alone at night without attendants and a lighted path to guide her every step.

The cool breeze wafting over the river made her shiver as the boat bumped with a dull thud against the landing quay.

"Stay in the boat," she whispered to Sitra, and patted the dagger that hung from her waist, concealed by the folds of her tunic. "I have this to protect me."

"But—"

"I'm not asking. I'm *ordering* you, Sitra! If you don't stay, the boatman might not wait for me."

As she stepped onto the ramp, Nefertiti saw the paving had not been swept since the celebration of Gempaaten. The walkway was still strewn with bits and pieces dropped by the crowd. Squashed food. Horse droppings. A shred of ribbon. A broken rush sandal left lying just as it had been dropped.

She thought of the sunlight and the crowds and the light reflecting off the gold and silver chariots. Now the long walkway stretching ahead in the moonlight between the shadowed faces of the ram-headed sphinxes seemed strangely daunting. Sinister.

She walked slowly, sensing the unblinking eyes of the sphinxes staring at her from either side. Every now and again she glanced back over her shoulder in case someone was following, her footsteps getting faster and faster and echoing against the paving, until she was almost running.

What if she were wrong? What if she had misunderstood the message? What if Tuthmosis had something else in mind? All this secrecy . . . what was it for?

A thought hit her and stopped her as sharply as if someone had pulled her back with a harness.

What if this was a trap?

If Tuthmosis had wanted to capture Amenhotep, he would have planned it differently.

There was only one answer for this secrecy.

Tuthmosis planned to *murder* Amenhotep!

As if in answer to this thought, she caught a movement from the corner of her eye. A shadow dropped down from a stone wall, dark, swift, and silent. It disappeared into a pool of darkness.

It *had* to be Tuthmosis.

Who else would be creeping about so stealthily? Surely not Amenhotep?

She shrank back against a pillar and waited. The shadow emerged again and paused on the palely lit steps, then disappeared between the pillars into the deep cavern of the Temple of Amun. Now the same steps where they had all stood at the celebration of Gempaaten were empty.

There was only one option. To reach the Sacred Lake inside the walled complex, she'd have to enter the temple and follow the sound of footfalls through the darkness.

25

THE SACRED LAKE

Nefertiti had gone only a few paces into the temple when she realized it was completely hopeless. The slight glimmer of moonlight coming in from the doorway dissolved into thick darkness. And the starlight entering far above through the small openings near ceiling height barely reached through the forest of massive columns.

The person might be anywhere. Maybe he was

standing only a few paces away, watching her. Perhaps even as close as the nearest column.

A shiver passed down her spine. She should have insisted that Sitra come with her.

The sound of breathing made her heart leap like a flame caught in a draft. She stood, as still as a statue, not daring to take a breath herself. The person was close. So close that maybe a hand would touch her.

But who? Tuthmosis or Amenhotep? Even if she'd tried to whisper a name, she couldn't have. Her throat had closed. She couldn't utter a sound.

There was a soft swish of rush sandals against stone. The person was moving away. She waited until the sound disappeared.

It was safer to cling to the side walls instead of following directly through the dark space of the temple, where she might bump into whoever it was. With her fingers trailing along the wall, she groped her way to the southern side door that led out to the Sacred Lake.

As she came out into the open, the moonlight seemed too bright. The silvery surface of the lake appeared like a huge expanse of cracked glass.

She ducked into the shadow of a pillar and stood with her back flattened against it. What if someone was watching her from the walls? Her throat tightened. Now she wished the mist would come back down.

The moonlight and shadows played tricks on her eyes. Every rustle, every movement, seemed like a person. She narrowed her eyes to focus.

Yes, someone was already standing alongside the huge carved scarab beetle at the edge of the moon-splintered lake.

Tuthmosis or Amenhotep? It was hard to tell from such a distance.

If it was Amenhotep, she should go forward and warn him. But what if she got there and found herself face-to-face with Tuthmosis? What then?

An owl swooped down from somewhere. The sharp cry of its prey ended in a strangled screech. An uneasy silence followed. A movement made her turn.

It was the shadow again . . . slinking forward and creeping toward the figure standing at the lake.

A shiver passed through her. Surely it wasn't Amenhotep. Why would he steal up like this?

The shadow had to be Tuthmosis and it was Amenhotep standing at the scarab.

She had to act. She had to warn Amenhotep.

She crouched low, felt for the dagger beneath her tunic, and drew it slowly out of its sheath. "Sekhmet, fill me with your lion spirit. Be beside me tonight."

The hardness of the ivory handle in her hand and the sharpness of the double-sided blade as she ran her thumb over it gave her strength. She crept forward.

The silhouettes of the two men were sharply outlined against the silver lake, but it was impossible to know which was Amenhotep and which Tuthmosis.

There was the merest flicker. But still a movement. An object glinted. The quickest flash of light. There was a single utterance like an explosion of breath.

Nefertiti sprang forward. A man staggered, then slowly dropped to his knees and crumpled at her feet.

"Amenhotep!" Her voice echoed against the stone walls. She heard the sound of it rise up, the breeze blowing it like a flapping pennant out over the water of the lake. "Amenhotep! Amenhotep!" She dropped down beside him and clutched his shoulders, wrapping him in her arms. "Amenhotep!"

Vaguely she sensed the shape of a man next to her. Then a breathless voice right up close. "Nefertiti, I'm here! I'm here beside you!"

"*Amenhotep?*" She flung her head back to stare up at him. Then looked back at the person she was cradling. "But . . ."

Amenhotep was staring down at her. "Nefertiti, you've blood on your hands! Are you hurt?" He grabbed hold of her, then pulled back sharply as he saw the person she was holding. "*What?* Nefertiti, what have you done?"

"*Done?* I've done nothing! It was *you*, Amenhotep! I saw you plunge the dagger into him! But the darkness muddled me. I didn't know who was who. I thought he had killed *you!* That this was you lying on the ground."

"Me? I've just come." He bent down quickly and lifted the shoulders of the man.

The arms fell limply back, but the face made pale by the moonlight was that of Tuthmosis.

"*Tuthmosis!*" Amenhotep spun around to face her. "Nefertiti, may the gods deliver us. What have you done? You've killed my brother!"

"*Me?*" She stepped back. "It was *you* who killed him! I thought it was Tuthmosis who'd plunged the dagger into you. *You* that Tuthmosis had killed. But it was the other way around. *You* killed him! It was *your* dagger!"

Amenhotep stooped and cradled the body of Tuthmosis against him and pressed his hand hard against the wound in his brother's chest. But in the moonlight Nefertiti saw the blood run freely and gather quickly, dark and almost black in a pool on the paving beneath him. And when Amenhotep held his cheek to Tuthmosis's face, she knew he'd feel no breath.

Amenhotep flung his head back and stared at her, his eyes like glassy stones glittering in the moonlight. "Tuthmosis came to make peace, not war! Why have you done this?"

"Me? You blame *me*? It wasn't *my* dagger that killed him. My blade is clean. I swear! I came here to protect you."

Amenhotep jumped up and took her by the shoulders and shook her. "If not your blade, then whose? *Whose* work is this? Tell me! Who was the person you brought with you to do this terrible thing? Tell me!"

Nefertiti pushed him away from her. "Believe me. I brought no one here. I was alone. I left my maid at the boat with the boatman."

"But there was a third person here. Didn't you see him? I thought he'd injured you."

"I saw no one except a shadow that I thought was Tuthmosis."

Amenhotep swung around and stared over his shoulder. "When you were crouching down, there was a person running. Didn't you see him?"

"You're not making sense."

"Someone ran swiftly past me just as I arrived."

"Then, it was *he* who killed Tuthmosis."

26

THE FUNERARY
BARGE

The cortege began its slow movement from the steps of the Temple of Amun through the avenue of sphinxes to the quayside. The procession walked in silence. The somber mood of the people had hushed even the children and city dogs.

So silent. How could a procession of so many people be so utterly quiet?

Far ahead, beyond the bobbing clay-covered heads

of the priests, Isikara caught sight of the brilliant splashes of red plumes in the crowns of Amenhotep and Nefertiti. They led the procession in separate carrying chairs of ebony and gold set with precious stones that glinted in the sunlight.

Isikara had been called on in the early hours of the morning to dye the white plumes red, to mark a time of mourning. She'd used alkanet dye from a recipe she'd known when she'd been a fletcher and had made arrows for the Nubian bowmen.

In the desert she had dyed feathers for the arrows of her brother, Katep, and her friend Anoukhet. Also for Tuthmosis.

Now she could barely breathe his name.

In Nubia she'd dyed the feathers for his arrows blue, to mark his royal birth—a color worthy of someone who should have worn the blue Khepresh warrior crown of Egypt. And now never would.

Her hands were stained red with alkanet. Red, as if stained with Tuthmosis's very own blood. And even though she'd washed and washed them, as if in the washing she could scrub away the horrible deed, the red had remained to remind her that someone else's hands were stained too. But with Tuthmosis's actual blood.

Tuthmosis was dead.

Who had wished him dead? Wosret? Amenhotep? Nefertiti? Perhaps even Nefertiti's maid? The gods knew they'd each had reason.

Which of them had plunged the dagger into his chest?

In the early dawn, long before the sky goddess, Nut, had plucked the sun from the east, the news had spread. In the sleeping city of Thebes people woke to cries of anguish that echoed across the Great River. Soft wails of mourning and the hollow rattling of sistrums replaced the cries. Women throughout the city raised their arms in sorrow, and the men of Thebes sank slowly to their knees and began sprinkling dust over their heads. As dawn broke as red as a bloodstain, the people tied white bands of mourning around their foreheads.

Isikara's throat had been too tight to utter a single sound. Her hands had worked numbly, steeping the feathers in the red dye in the yard of the unguent rooms. She'd hung them to dry in the hot wind that had sprung up from the desert at sunrise. Intef had stood silently by, bringing a comfort more than words, and Ta-Miu had sat quietly in a corner.

Now the cortege moved slowly forward. A heat haze was gathering in the distance in the tomb-riddled landscape of the Theban hills.

The tomb entrances faced east so that the rising sun would wake the dead from their sleep. But Tuthmosis would never be woken. Not in this world while she was still alive. When he went to meet Maat and Thoth at the weighing scales, his heart would be light, but not light enough to return to her in Thebes.

Hathor, Lady of the West, had stolen him forever.

The shadows of the sphinxes cast long stripes across the procession as it shuffled forward. The sun beat down, and the smell of myrrh and incense from the smoking censers made the air hotter. Isikara felt the sand chafing between her toes and sandals and was grateful for the wind that blew through her robes.

Through a gap in the crowd Isikara saw past the priests and female mourners and caught sight of the body being carried by bearers on its lion-pawed bier. Two falcon-headed priestesses walked alongside, one at the head, the other at the foot. Just as the goddesses Isis and Nephthys had walked with their brother Osiris.

From so far back in the procession, Isikara couldn't see Tuthmosis's face. It was impossible to believe he was *truly* dead. The first time she'd ever seen him, he'd been lying in his leopard cloak on the stone bed in the wabet chamber. She'd thought him dead then. Wosret had poisoned him. But her father had saved him.

Wosret! His name choked her.

The bier was set down at the quay, with the red plumes of Nefertiti and Amenhotep drawing everyone's eyes toward it.

Alongside the quay the unpainted funerary barge was strewn with lilies and lotus flowers. It waited to take Tuthmosis's body to the Southern Opet Temple to be blessed before the body was taken to the wabet chamber for embalming. This time he hadn't been poisoned. He would not wake up.

She needed to see his face. She pushed ahead to catch one final glimpse of him.

He lay with his piercing blue eyes closed, his lips quiet, his hair dressed in a short Nubian wig. A gold bird with a human head spread its wings protectively over his chest. It was the amulet for his soul that fluttered above him. Its outstretched wings, studded with precious stones, masked any sign of a wound.

The two falcon-headed priestesses were chanting and calling his soul to return to his body. "Come for my soul, O guardians of the heavens! May it rest in my body so that it will never be destroyed."

When she saw him again after seventy days of lying in the wabet chamber, he would be hidden from her. Wrapped in layers and layers of linen, with his face hidden behind a golden mummy mask, his body sealed within a mummy case. Oxen would draw his sledge into the Theban hills. Musicians and dancers would lead the way.

Finally the mummy case would be placed in the stone sarcophagus in the burial chamber.

Silent and alone in the darkness.

And the tomb would be sealed.

She shuddered now as the drummer began a slow drumbeat.

Tuthmosis's body was lifted on the bier and placed in the flower-strewn barge to begin the journey.

She gave a last look at his silent face.

Around her the women mourners set up their desolate cries. Along the riverbanks people knelt and touched their dust-strewn heads to the ground.

Children scattered lotus flowers that perfumed the air and floated on the water in the path of the barge, as the slow dip of the oars joined the women's dreadful lament.

27
THE TEMPLE OF OPET

K iya and I were pushed along by the jostling crowds of mourners and women rattling sistrums in our faces. It was hot beyond words. A billowing cloud of yellow dust sweeping in from the desert had turned the sunlight to copper. Dust scoured my eyes and throat, and sand stuck to my skin.

Today the loaves of unleavened bread for a time

of mourning would be sprinkled not just with flour, but with the grit of Egypt.

By the time the barge reached the Southern Opet Temple, I caught sight of Isikara and edged my way toward her. A shadow had settled on her face. Her eyes were red-rimmed, not just from the sand.

"Isikara?" My voice sounded shaky and not my own.

She pulled a linen veil across her face to keep out the dust.

"You should've stayed behind to grieve in quiet. Don't follow into the temple. Wait here with Kiya. I'll bring you both something to drink. Stay close to the statue of Hathor. I'll see what I can find."

I hurried through the crowds, hoping to see someone selling pomegranate juice.

"There she is!" A voice came from behind me as I shouldered my way through the people. "It's that moonstruck girl. Haven't seen *her* in a while."

I twisted around. It was one of the old sweeping ladies from the temple.

"They say she's been in prison."

"Hmmph! Prison hasn't done much for her looks.

There'll be no boys running after her until she puts some flesh on those bones."

"You'd have to spend a lifetime in prison to lose all *your* flesh, Meryt."

"A frog in your mouth, Senen! I've seen no sign of her lazy boyfriend lately. They say . . ." The voices trailed off, lost in a hubbub of noise.

They say *what*? Did they have news of Samut?

I craned my neck to see the direction they'd taken, but in the throng of people, it was all I could do to stay upright without my feet tripping up beneath me.

Suddenly a voice growled into my ear. "Traitor!"

I turned swiftly and nearly fell. There was a strong grip on my arm, not so much to keep me from falling as to inflict pain.

"Let go of me!" I yelled, then looked straight up into the eyes of Samut.

"*Samut!* Samut, where have you been?" Without thinking, I thumped my fists into his chest. "Why didn't you come for me?"

He wrenched my fists away. "Stay away from me!"

"What? What have I done? I've been in prison. Why didn't you come to have me freed?" I hammered at him again.

He grabbed my hands and flung them away. "Don't touch me."

"Have you gone mad? You left me in prison. *Where* have you been? Wosret wants you arrested."

"I'm still free . . . as you can see! But not because of you!" A small muscle twitched at the side of his jaw. "You betrayed me." He turned away abruptly.

"Wait!" I grabbed hold of his arm and pulled him back. "You can't leave until you've heard my side. I didn't purposely betray you! You *must* believe me. I kept silent while I waited for you to come to me in prison. I spoke out only after they said Isikara would be blinded. All I did was speak the truth. I told them you'd given me the ring. I said no more than that. I didn't say you'd stolen the ring. You *must* understand."

I stared into his eyes. There was no spark of warmth in them.

"You told them I knew about the key."

"But I didn't say you *used* the key. You must understand. I was forced to speak out."

"I do understand. Our friendship counted for nothing. Tuthmosis was more important to you. You pretended you cared for me, but the moment he returned to Thebes, you betrayed me, hoping he'd come rushing to your side."

"I *never* betrayed you! I never said you entered the tomb. How could I? I didn't know for sure. All I said was that you knew about the key. And why do you speak badly of Tuthmosis, when he has been murdered? May Horus protect you." I quickly drew a wedjat eye in the sand with the toe of my sandal. "Have you no respect?"

"Respect!" Samut hissed. "For someone like Tuthmosis!" He spat at my feet. "What respect should I have for Tuthmosis, with his churlish manners and disdainful ways, behaving like a god?"

"Tuthmosis wasn't churlish!"

"Hah! Protect him as much as you like. Neither he nor his father showed *me* any respect."

"You? What were you to them?"

"What do you care?"

I eyed him. This hard, glowering face was one I didn't know. "You're jealous."

"Jealous? Of their wealth? Or because you cared for him? Well, I'm *not!* With every breath in my body I hated him!"

"*Hated?* How can you speak like this when he is hardly dead?"

"Hardly dead? Believe me, Tuthmosis is *very* dead."

Samut stared at me with eyes as cold and hard as black onyx. For a moment my breath caught. "*You?* Samut . . . ?" I could hardly find the words. "What are you talking of? Did you . . . ?"

"*Kill* Tuthmosis?" he sneered. "Do you think I'd tell? So you can run off to Amenhotep and report it? You and your precious Kiya—Princess Tadukhepa— Isikara and Nefertiti as well . . . are all traitors!"

"Samut, don't speak like that! We *are* innocent."

"Don't think Nefertiti's innocent."

I stared at him. "What are you saying? You mean *she* killed Tuthmosis?"

"Nefertiti's too clever for that! She'd never dirty her hands. She wouldn't risk her place with Amenhotep. But she's cunning. She stops at nothing to have her own way. She thought one beckon from her would have me at her side."

"What are you talking of?"

"She tried to flirt with me."

"What?"

Samut laughed. "Surprised? Yes. At the stables."

"The stables?" I stared back at him, taking in every detail of his expression. His lips and eyes were as hard as onyx that had once sparkled. My arms dropped to my sides. I nodded like someone in a dream. "I do believe you. You hate us all."

An ugly sneer spread across his mouth.

The spirit of Sekhmet suddenly entered me. I flung myself at him, leaped at his throat, and dug my fingers into his neck. "It was *you*, wasn't it? It was you who plunged the dagger into Tuthmosis! You *murderer!*"

28

POISON

"Ta-Miu, where have you been?" Someone was shaking me. I stared back at the girl in front of me. Then I realized it was Isikara.

"Ta-Miu? I've been searching everywhere for you. I waited, but you didn't come. Kiya is frantic with worry. The procession is over."

Her words ran together. I looked down at my hands. There was blood and dirt under my fingernails. My thoughts were as murky as the dust-filled air.

She sat down on the riverbank next to me. "Ta-Miu, what's happened? Are you ill?"

I turned my head away so as not to meet her eyes.

Isikara's papyrus had said everything. I had read *every* single word of it. The one she had planned to show Amenhotep. She had pushed it into my hands without speaking in the early hours of this morning, after we'd heard of Tuthmosis's murder.

While she'd swirled red dye around and around in a stone basin, and Intef had stood nearby as if watching, I'd sat in a corner with the sky barely light and had read on and on. As the stars had paled, the words had become clearer and clearer. Finally the very last sentence had appeared—

May anyone who reads these words know they are written by the feather of truth under the protection of the Eye of the Moon.

I had sat in silence and watched the slow drip of red fall from the feathers as Isikara hung them out to dry.

She hadn't needed to speak. I knew from all she had written that she'd truly loved Tuthmosis.

Now I couldn't meet her eyes. I twisted away from her. "Leave me alone."

"Ta-Miu, we are *all* mourning Tuthmosis."

I nodded. "Yes . . . but *I* . . ."

"You what?"

The words came out as a whisper. "I caused his death."

Isikara flinched. The shadow was back on her face. "What? *You* plunged the dagger into Tuthmosis?"

I shook my head so vigorously I felt the plaits of my wig swing against my neck. "No! *Never!*"

"Then, what?"

"*Samut* killed Tuthmosis."

"Samut? Don't be foolish. Why would he draw attention to himself? He's already on the run for having stolen the ring."

"I saw him."

"You *saw* him murder Tuthmosis? Why didn't you speak out before?"

"No. I saw him in the crowd."

I buried my head against my knees to blot out Samut's expression. It was the look of a wild animal. Not the Samut I knew. I spoke into the fabric of my tunic. "He seemed demented."

"Did he admit to it?"

"He rambled on about Kiya and Nefertiti and

me. He said he hated Tuthmosis. Hated us all. I attacked him then."

"For the love of Horus, Ta-Miu, what did you do?" Isikara grabbed hold of my hands. "You've blood on your hands. Have you *killed* Samut?"

I pulled away from her. "I wish I had. I tried to throttle him for that sneer on his face. But I wasn't strong enough. He laughed at me." I sank my head to my knees again. "Now *you* must hate me too."

There was silence as we sifted through our thoughts, looking for the bits that made sense.

Isikara stayed quiet for such a long time that I turned to glance at her. She was staring at the river, watching some fishermen in reed boats throw nets into the water. She plucked absently at a piece of reed. A red dragonfly touched lightly against the back of her neck like the exotic clasp of a necklace.

Then she sighed as if she needed to fill her lungs with air. "Boats seem too frail to stay afloat. But they're stronger than you think. Our boat took us against the current nearly to the First Cataract at Syene. A long journey, and an even longer one coming home, from the farthest parts of Nubia all the way back to Thebes."

I picked up a handful of pebbles and hurled them into the water. "Don't speak like this! I know about your journey with Tuthmosis."

"Tuthmosis returned to Thebes for a reason. To make peace."

I squinted back at her. "I know. I don't want to be reminded. I know how much you loved him." I took hold of her hands. "Isikara, I beg you, listen. I know you can never forgive me, but I need one last favor. Do you know the recipe for making poison?"

Isikara glanced sharply at me. *"Poison?"*

"Will you tell me?"

"It's complex. The exact measure of snake's venom has to be correct. If the mixture is too dilute, death is slow and horrible. It's not as easy as making a mixture of fat for rubbing into the scalp to cure baldness, or making a powder of ground skull of catfish fried in oil, for whooping cough." She narrowed her eyes at me. *"Who* do you plan to poison?"

"Myself."

Her eyebrows shot high.

"It's the only way. Will you mix a poison but blend it with honey and milk so my throat won't know?"

"Don't be stupid!"

"But how can I live knowing Samut killed Tuthmosis because of me?"

Isikara tossed her head. "Do you think I would mix a poison to help you die? Why should I?"

"I know you hate me. But I beg you, Isikara. I'm not brave enough to plunge a dagger into my heart, or hold a viper to my throat, or throw myself to crocodiles. I know you can't forgive me. But have enough pity to do this last thing for me."

"You don't believe Samut committed murder because of *you!*"

"Why else?"

"Samut is too selfish. He's never done anything for anyone. You heard the stories in the unguent rooms. He didn't even steal the ring especially for you. He might just as easily have given it to another girl. He flirted with them all."

"You don't know this for sure."

"Are you defending a murderer? Don't be foolish, Ta-Miu. He did this for another reason. And the only one I can think of is that *Wosret* was part of this plan."

"How?"

"Wosret wanted Tuthmosis out of the way. Tuthmosis came back to Thebes to speak out against him.

If Samut wielded the dagger, it was Wosret who gave the order." She shook her head. "No, I won't make a poison for you. Your job is to tell Amenhotep and Nefertiti what Samut said."

"I can't."

"You *have* to! You've spoken out against him before. The second time will be easier. Or ask Kiya to do it for you."

29

THE CHEETAHS

Amenhotep glanced at Kiya. "Is this true?"

Kiya bowed. "By the feather of Maat, I speak the truth. Ta-Miu was too upset to come herself."

Nefertiti narrowed her eyes. "Why would your serving girl accuse Samut of murder? She's protected him in the past."

"Her friendship was misplaced. She knows this now."

Nefertiti's eyebrow shot up. "Too late. Her friend-ship has caused Tuthmosis's death."

Kiya shook her head. "Isikara believes Wosret was behind the murder."

Nefertiti tossed her head so that her earrings jangled. "Why should we believe Isikara? She has no position in Thebes."

Amenhotep turned to her. "I believe what Tuthmosis wrote in his letter. The power of the priests is too great. We must call Wosret and the two girls so that we can hear the truth."

He had hardly spoken when Wosret himself hurried into the hall and bowed breathlessly before Amenhotep and Nefertiti. The cheetahs sprawled out on red cushions on the floor alongside Nefertiti lifted their heads at the disturbance. "My lord and lady, I rushed to your side immediately on hearing the news."

Amenhotep inclined his head. "What news, Wosret?"

"Samut is the murderer."

"Who told you?"

Wosret waved his arms about. "News travels faster than dust." He went on breathlessly. "I've dealt with it. I've sent out guards to search for Samut. This is *inconceivable*. Someone so evil that he would kill the brother of a king!"

"Have you arrested him?"

Wosret shook his head. "Samut can't be found. He seems to have escaped from Thebes."

Amenhotep frowned. "Escaped?"

Wosret nodded. "It proves his guilt. Nor can the girls be found."

Kiya looked up sharply. "Isikara and Ta-Miu? That's impossible. I left them a moment ago in my quarters."

"And now they're gone!" Wosret shrugged and clicked his fingers as if some magic had been called upon to make them disappear so quickly. Then he bowed to Amenhotep and Nefertiti again. "On the evening of your brother's funeral, you shouldn't cope with such matters. Leave it to me. I'll send soldiers beyond Thebes and have Samut found and punished. It needs someone of experience in these matters."

Amenhotep shook his head. "What I can't understand is why you didn't arrest Samut when we first discovered he was the tomb robber."

"He disappeared then, too. But now we know he's not just a tomb robber but a murderer."

"Are you experienced in matters of murder?"

Wosret seemed taken by surprise. His hand stopped in midair. Then he quickly regained his composure. "There are murders in Thebes all the time."

"And poisonings?"

"Poisonings?" He shrugged his shoulders and narrowed his eyes at Amenhotep, as if he wished he could click his fingers and the king *too* would be gone. "I know nothing of poisonings. I refer to murders committed by rogues who want the downfall of Egypt. I'm loyal to Egypt and serve you in the best possible way. Of this you can be assured."

"Your loyalty is in doubt."

"In doubt?" Wosret's eyes darted from Amenhotep to Nefertiti. "What do you mean? How can you doubt me, the highest of high priests? I was mentor to your brother, Tuthmosis . . . may Hathor carry his soul into the west." He bowed low. "And a mentor to you as well."

"There's too much secrecy between the priests. I've decided to make changes."

"Changes?"

"From now on temples will be open to every Egyptian, so worship and rituals can be observed by all. There'll be no more secret inner sanctum. Aten's light will be allowed to shine into it."

"Aten? What about the gods Amun, Mut, and Khonsu? Their rituals are private. A matter between the gods and the priests only. Every day in the inner sanctum they are begged and placated by my priests. How else do you think we keep the god of chaos away?"

Amenhotep shook his head. "We've lived too long by secret rituals. Aten's light will keep away the god of chaos. The light of the sun disk will banish darkness from our minds and hearts."

Wosret flung his arms upward. "This is blasphemous. How can you allow common peasants to observe secret rituals? *You*, the son of a king, speak like this!"

"Not the *son* of a king. You forget Wosret, I *am* the king. Appointed by you."

"Exactly!" Wosret spun around with his arms spread wide. "Nefertiti!" The cheetahs growled from their cushions at his sudden movement. Wosret made a slight movement to kick at the nearest one but then seemed to think better of it. "Nefertiti, I appeal to you. Talk sense into your husband. Your child will be born into a land of chaos. If the gods aren't there to protect us, Egypt will fall to her enemies."

Nefertiti gazed at him and shook her head. "You forget your place, Wosret. I must listen to my husband."

"*What?*" Wosret's mouth took on an ugly sneer. "You've never listened to anyone! I thought I could guide you, but you are the most willful person I know. I've covered up for you for too long."

He swung abruptly to face Amenhotep. "What do you say to finding your wife with a dagger in her hands over the body of your brother? If you are looking for the *real* murderer, don't look for Samut. Look no farther than to the one who sits on the throne right beside you."

Nefertiti leaped up. "How dare you!" Her cheetahs sprang from their cushions and snarled.

"As the highest of high priests it's my duty. I'm trying to protect you *both* from scandal. None of what I've said will leave this hall." He bowed toward Amenhotep. "I'll protect you from the scandal of your wife's part in your brother's murder. But in return I must remain and the Priests of Amun must remain."

Amenhotep shook his head. "There's no scandal, Wosret. I was there. I know what happened. Nefertiti is not the murderer. Her blade was clean. There wasn't a drop of blood on it."

Wosret moved in closer, took Amenhotep by the arm, and spoke in a voice that dripped with honey. "You're mistaken. She could have wiped it clean. Think of this. What was she doing next to the Sacred Lake so late at night? She needed no extra motivation to commit the murder. She'd already confessed to me that she hated Tuthmosis for returning to take your throne." He swung around and pointed at Nefertiti. "Ask *her*, not Samut, about Tuthmosis's death. I was ready to make Samut a scapegoat. To blame it on him to avoid a royal scandal. But *she* is the true murderer."

Nefertiti's eyes glittered, as hard as gemstones. "You'll regret this!"

Amenhotep shook his head. "You can't persuade me, Wosret. You twist things around this way and that like a washerwoman wringing out linen. But I read my brother's note and believe him. You know what was written. You read the note as well."

"Your private note? How was *I* to read it?"

"Because it disappeared from a locked chest and was found shredded near your quarters by a serving girl. If you've sent guards out after Samut, why do you accuse my wife?"

"I told you. I sent guards after Samut to prevent a scandal."

"I don't believe you. You're hiding the truth behind a haze of smoke. I no longer trust you. I'm taking away the power of the Priests of Amun. The temples will have Amun's name removed. The name of Aten will be carved in its place."

"You can't deface the temples, the very holiest of holy places! I *forbid* it!"

"You can't forbid it! Aten is the god of light who has no secrecy. No hidden places. He needs no helpers to do his work. The Priests of Amun are no longer needed. This is the start of a new religion in Egypt."

Wosret made a quick gesture. He grabbed something from his girdle and lunged forward. In a blur both cheetahs sprang and knocked him to the floor. A dagger went spinning across the hard tiles. A cheetah stood snarling with its forepaws firmly planted against

Wosret's lower body. The other cheetah lay crouched against his chest, its lips pulled back in a snarl. Its exposed fangs hovered at the base of Wosret's throat.

There was absolute silence, as if a nest of scorpions had paralyzed the throats of everyone who stood there. Not even an eyebrow moved as every person held their breath and looked on with unblinking eyes. The only sounds were the low threatening growls of the cheetahs.

Wosret lay beneath their paws, his hands and legs spread stiffly against the hard tiled floor. His eyes were tightly closed. His jaw rigid. Except for the small rise and fall of his chest, he lay as someone already dead.

The cheetah at Wosret's throat snarled and lowered its head so that its fangs touched against the flesh of his neck. Nefertiti had only to give the command and Wosret's life would end.

No one moved.

It was Nefertiti who recovered first. Kiya saw her exchange glances with Amenhotep. Something seemed to pass between them without either speaking. Then she nodded as if a decision had been made. She made a soft sound in the back of her throat and snapped her fingers. "Come here, you two!"

The cheetahs raised their heads and looked back at her, their paws still resting heavily against Wosret. Then slowly and languidly they rose from their crouched positions and stood on either side of Wosret, their lips pulled back, panting and staring unblinkingly around the room as if loath to leave their prey.

Nefertiti stepped forward and looked down at Wosret. With the toe of her sandal she flicked her foot against the cheetahs' haunches. "Come now! Enough! Leave this man alone. There are tastier meals. His flesh is poisoned with the venom of his evil ways. He's not worth eating."

The cheetahs turned and padded quietly to her side. There was an audible sigh as everyone breathed out again.

It took a while longer for life to flow back into Wosret. He opened his eyes slowly and raised his hands to explore his throat, as if checking that his neck were still in one piece. Then he got to his feet, stood stiffly, and spoke through tight lips. "You'll regret the day you allowed your animals to threaten the highest of high priests of not only Thebes, but all Egypt." He swept his gaze between Amenhotep and Nefertiti. "You are mere figureheads. Remember it is

I who appointed you both, *I* who control Egypt, and *I* who hold the power. The Priests of Amun can't be pushed aside. The two of you won't spoil my plans. I have the power to silence *all* who get in my way . . . just as I silenced Tuthmosis."

Amenhotep stepped forward. "So it's true! You ordered Samut to kill my brother."

Wosret looked triumphantly around the hall. "No one can prove it."

"Princess Tadukhepa's maid and Isikara will testify against you. And Samut will be found for his version of the story."

Wosret shook his head. "You're too late! You'll not find them. Neither the girls nor Samut. They've been dealt with."

"Dealt with?" Kiya stepped forward. "What have you done to Ta-Miu and Isikara?"

Nefertiti's eyes glittered. "I don't regret allowing my cheetahs to attack you. But I *do* regret not letting them finish the job. Arrest him, Amenhotep."

30

THE LABYRINTH

We were at the gate of the labyrinth. I wrenched myself free of the guard holding me. "Why are we being held captive? Why have you brought us here? I demand to know."

"Demand?" the guard sneered. "You aren't in a position to demand anything."

"Don't you know who we are? I'm maid to Princess Tadukhepa, who is one of the king's royal wives, and my friend is Isikara, daughter of the priest at the Temple of Sobek."

The man glanced across at his fellow guard and shrugged. "The names mean nothing to us."

I gave him a look. He was more boy than man, with a fuzzy growth of hair sprouting from above his top lip. "Surely the king means something to you!"

The guard shrugged. "We take our orders not from the king but from the highest of high priests. He ordered us to bring you here."

"Wosret?" I caught the look in Isikara's eyes.

The guard nodded at me. "Now unlock the gate."

I bit my lip, trying to think of anything that would delay us. "Find the duplicate key!"

"You know that's gone. Stolen from the shelf by your friend." He twisted my arm behind my back. "Now hand over your key."

"If I don't?"

"You'll regret it," he sneered. "It won't be all you'll regret today. Now, stop delaying." His fingers gripped the gold cord around my neck and pulled. I felt it cut into my flesh. He bent close to my ear. "Hand over the key or this nice little neck of yours might be harmed. Do you hear me?"

"Give it to him, Ta-Miu," Isikara urged.

I removed the cord from my neck and handed him the key.

"That's better." He twisted it in the lock. The gate swung open. Then he pushed us forward. The two guards followed close behind.

"My key." I held out my hand. "Give it back!"

A small twitch of amusement crossed the guard's lips. "Feisty, aren't you? You're not getting it back." He pulled me close toward him, so close I could smell his foul breath.

"Let go of me!" I jabbed my elbow into his ribs.

Isikara wrenched herself free from her guard and swung her fist into the shoulder of the one holding me. "You heard her! Let go of her, you oaf!"

"Oaf, is it?" He moved threateningly toward Isikara.

I tried to distract him. "What are you going to do to us?" I asked.

"Put it this way," he sneered. "You've seen your last ray of sunshine . . . ever!"

"Don't speak in riddles!" Isikara snarled.

"Mind your tongue, girl! We're taking you to King Amenhotep's burial chamber."

I felt my breath catch. "Why?"

"Why do people get taken to burial chambers?" A small smirk crossed his face as he watched us staring at him. He nodded. "Yes. You're going on a journey."

"A journey?"

"A journey to the afterlife. You're going to die. It's as simple as that! Wosret commands it."

I shook my head. "You don't have to do everything Wosret commands."

"Don't confuse things. We've been given orders. We have to carry them out."

The other guard shook his head. "Let's get going. These ones put on airs and graces as if they're Nefertiti themselves. I can't bear the likes of them. Let's hurry. Do what we have to do. I want to get home."

My guard grabbed my arm and pushed me hard in the back, almost making me fall.

"Leave her!"

It was a man's voice. Suddenly the outline of two figures appeared in the gateway. I narrowed my eyes to focus against the light. One was a guard, and the other was . . . Could it be?

"Samut?"

"It's him, all right!" the guard sneered. "But don't

get any ideas. He's not here to save you. His fate is the same as yours. Get along." Before I had a chance to speak, the one with the sprouting top lip pushed me forward. "We've waited too long for this other fellow. There's no more time to waste." He pushed the gate sharply shut behind Samut and his guard and twisted the key in the lock. Then he slipped the key into his girdle bag.

"Get going now!" He took the lamp the other guard had lit and held it so that the light flickered ahead into the darkness.

Samut was silent.

Isikara glared at the guard. "The labyrinth is vast. Do you know where you're going?"

The guard grinned back at her. "Yes. And I know you've been here before. You helped Tuthmosis. Now see where it's gotten you!" He nodded his head toward Samut. "And he knows the way too. So we won't be getting lost!"

"I don't regret helping Tuthmosis. And you haven't answered. Where are you taking us?"

"To the well that blocks the passageway leading into the king's burial chamber."

"The well?" Isikara looked across at me. She had

written about the well in her papyrus. It had smooth sides and no footholds and was deep. I felt my throat close up, and I fought to fill my lungs with air, as if I were already drowning.

Isikara managed a scornful look. "Water doesn't bother me. I'm a good swimmer."

"A good swimmer! Hah! Not when there's no river-bank to swim to. No footholds to help you out. Just slippery sides that will keep you in there going around and around like a rat trying to get out of a beer vat."

Words dried up in my throat. The labyrinth ceiling seemed to push down on me. I could hardly draw breath.

Isikara might have been a good swimmer. She'd lived next to the Great River. But I wasn't. When Kiya and I had come from Mitanni, the horsemen had taken us across the rivers on their horses. At the deepest places the horses had swum, with us desperately clinging to their necks. I'd drown the moment I was thrown into the well. I wouldn't last even as long as a rat.

And why? All because of Samut . . . Samut . . . who was walking in silence behind us.

We passed through a confusion of passageways that twisted this way and that, with enormous paintings of gods. But I was too distracted to notice properly. At times Anubis glared down at us. At other times Amenhotep. And once, Nut was above, sprinkling gold stars down from the vaulted ceiling. But it was all a blur. Even creatures scuttling across my foot meant nothing. My body was numb. My legs shuffled forward without knowing how.

Eventually we came to a dead end. One of the guards placed both palms against the stone wall. My eyes searched the gloom. For a moment nothing happened, and then an entire segment of wall swung open and shifted inward into a dark cavity.

A creature sat there . . . a stone statue of Anubis with eyes that blazed in the lamplight. My heartbeat quickened as we stepped past the statue through the opening into a passageway that led into a vast hall. A ceiling stretched high above us, and mysterious alcoves and passageways led away from the lamplight into utter blackness. The echoing sound of our footsteps told of how huge the space was.

"Be careful of how you tread!" Isikara whispered up close to me.

My guard lifted his lamp high. "There it is. The well."

I glanced down. My insides seemed to drop from me.

Right at our feet in a sharp bend of passageway was a deep shaft with sides of solid, smooth rock. A long narrow stone slab lay stretched across it, put there by someone . . . perhaps even by Samut when he was last in the tomb. Far, far below, the lamplight flickered against an oily black sheen of water.

The guard nodded again. "It's deep." He didn't have to say more. He picked up a small pebble from the stone floor and dropped it. There was a long drawn-out silence. When my ears felt they could stand it no longer, I finally heard the splash.

"*Very* deep!" He looked across at Isikara. "No matter how good a swimmer you are."

She shrugged. "What harm have we done you? Do you have to follow Wosret's orders so blindly like goats being led to the slaughtering post?"

I bit my lip thinking she'd used the wrong words. We were the goats being led to slaughter. When I glanced across at Samut, he wouldn't meet my eye.

"Shut your mouth!" a guard snapped at Isikara, but she was not to be stopped.

"Can't you show you are men and not boys?" There was scorn in her tone. "Men stand up for themselves. They make their own decisions about what is right or wrong. You know this is wrong. You know we're innocent."

"That may be so, but *he's* not." Samut's guard gave him a shake. "He murdered Tuthmosis."

Samut flung off his guard's hand and spoke for the first time. "I murdered him for a reason."

I looked across at him, scared for all of us by the strange look in his eyes. With one wild sweep of his arms he could've grabbed any one of us and pushed us into the well. Or jumped and pulled us with him. I tried to keep my voice calm. Tried to keep him talking. "Why, Samut?"

"Why?" His eyes blazed. "Because I hated both of them. Him *and* his father. They took away from me the only thing I truly loved . . . the horses."

The horses? I thought back to my evenings with him at the stables. Of course.

"I was a stable hand in the palace stables when Tuthmosis fell from his father's chariot and crushed his leg. Afterward the accident was blamed on me. The king said I hadn't harnessed his horses properly. I'd *never* have neglected this. But no one believed me. The king dismissed me from the stables."

"Tuthmosis never blamed his lameness on you." Isikara's voice was calm but hard. "He told me it was an accident. He said they were racing too fast. That the wheel hit a stone. He was jolted from the chariot and fell. His leg was crushed by the wheel."

"But his father blamed me. He was king. And Tuthmosis was to be king. I hated them both for taking what I loved away from me. I couldn't get work in any stable after that."

"You can't hate someone who's innocent. Tuthmosis probably didn't even know you'd lost your job," she said. I saw her clench her fists as if she had to prevent herself from giving Samut a hard push so that he'd fall backward into the well.

"Exactly! He didn't care. I was just the stable boy. But I suffered. And all the riches I stole from this tomb were only so I could disrupt his father's journey to the afterlife. I wanted the king punished. I didn't care anything for the jewels and gold. I gave it all away."

"Did you care for me?" I whispered.

Samut looked away.

"Samut?" I asked again.

"I did once. But the ankh around your neck reminded me of your friendship with Tuthmosis."

Isikara swept a look around at us all. "And now here we are and we must decide what must be done."

Done? I looked across at her. Had she gone mad? Why was she reminding the guards of what they were meant to be doing?

She nodded. "Surely we can decide this together."

Her guard shook his head and laughed. "What's to decide? The decision's already made. The three of you are to be thrown into the well. Wosret commands it."

Isikara laughed as if she thought him a fool. "That's a stupid idea, and you know it! Why would you commit a crime in such a sacred place? Why would you want to turn the well sour with our bodies? King Amenhotep's spirit would never rest. He'd never leave you in peace. When the three of you in turn die and it's time for you to travel on the ferryboat of Ra to the World of the Dead, Thoth will be waiting for you in the Hall of Maat with the Scales of Justice and will judge you. 'My heart is righteous,' is what he wants to hear. 'I am pure. I have done no evil in place of right and truth.'"

She paused and looked at each guard separately. "But will any of you be able to say it? Will you be able to speak? Or will your jaws clamp shut? When Anubis's eyes glow like burning coals and Ammut bares her teeth and her snout is bloody, will you be able to say 'I have not disobeyed the gods. I have not inflicted pain on anyone. I have not killed.' When your hearts are placed on the Scales of Justice, will they rise lighter than the feather? I don't think so!"

She stared at them as if putting a curse on them. "If you throw us down the well, there'll be no truth in your words. You'll be damned forever."

The guard holding her shrugged and looked around at the other two. "I've had enough of her. Let's shut her up for good! She can be the *first* to go!"

Samut took a step forward. "No! Push me in first. I'm not scared to die. Go on!" he challenged.

But my guard, the one with fuzz on his lip, was wide-eyed. "Wait. She's right. We won't be able to answer."

This was all Isikara needed. She plunged straight on as if she hadn't been interrupted. "No, you won't be able to say any of these things. And Ammut will snatch your hearts and drag them off. You'll be banned from the afterlife. Is that how you want it to be?"

"Let me shut her up. Her words are making me prickly, as if Ammut's breath were already on my neck."

"Do it, then, if you're so anxious to shut her up," said my guard.

"Isikara . . . stop!" I pulled her arm. Tried to stop her ranting.

She took no notice. "You are all fools. Do you want all three of our deaths on your hands just because Wosret demands it? Which of you will be brave enough to shove the first of us in?"

I squeezed my eyes shut. Held my breath.

No sound came. No one moved.

"He's the highest of high priests. How can we refuse him?" It was my guard speaking.

"Enough now!" Samut's guard nudged his friend. "She has far too much to say. Let's take action."

"Or you could leave us here," Isikara went on, her voice calm, not pleading, just firm. In the lamplight she looked innocent. But I knew better. It was a trap. She was playing a game, as though this were a board game and she were urging an unsuspecting opponent to make a move to help Isikara's piece reach the other side unharmed. "Go back. Say you've done the deed. Imagine how much better you'll sleep tonight. Innocent of murder."

One of the guards snorted. "And then?"

"Later we'll escape. We'll all three leave Thebes and never return. No one will bother to search for our bodies in the well. No one will ever know."

She made it seem so simple. As if anyone could have thought of it, even the guards, if they'd given themselves enough time. She was almost suggesting it was their idea in the first place.

"No one will know. You'll be innocent of murder. When you stand in front of Thoth, your hearts will rest lightly on the Scales of Justice. Thoth will reward you. Don't you believe a wise man would do this?"

No one spoke. The dark spaces were silent except for the echo of her words.

"No! Enough delaying!" Her guard jostled her forward.

I heard the sound of my voice echoing through the spaces as I screamed. Then everything happened too fast to understand the order.

Samut's arm went out and up. His fist struck Isikara's guard's chin so that the guard was flung back and hit the stone floor with a dull thud.

"Run!" Samut shouted at us. But we had turned to stone. Samut had already spun around and come thumping into the stomach of the second guard. He too fell to the floor, with a huge gasp of air leaving his body.

When the third guard sprang at Samut, they both fell to the floor and lay fighting with their fists. Then suddenly the guard managed to pull free. He jumped up and stood facing all three of us. Isikara wrenched me back from the edge of the well. But it was Samut he lunged at. Samut sidestepped. The guard slipped, and suddenly he overbalanced and began falling. And as he did, he thrust out a hand and grabbed.

He took Samut with him into the well.

With terrible curses they both disappeared over the edge into the darkness.

The splashes as the two bodies hit the water were much louder than the sound of a pebble.

I stood paralyzed.

I didn't want to look down and see them in that dark, oily water fighting for their lives . . . until each was too tired to keep his head above the surface.

But Isikara grabbed hold of the lamp that was on the floor and bent over the edge.

"He's dead." A muffled gasp came up to us as if from the end of a long tunnel. "He must've hit his head against the side as he fell."

It was Samut's voice.

I stood back, hardly daring to breathe. Watched Isikara looking down at Samut. Imagined his face pale in the lamplight far below. I waited for her to speak. But she said nothing. The moment seemed very long. I could hear the sound of Samut splashing.

Then Isikara turned and eyed me. "Which guard has your key?"

I stared, wide-eyed, back at her. The key! We needed the key to get out. The duplicate one inside the gate had been stolen by Samut, my guard had said. Why else had he wanted the key from around my neck?

I looked around desperately. Perhaps it was my guard who'd fallen into the well. But no, I suddenly remembered. He was the one with the fuzzy lip whom Isikara had almost persuaded. He lay there on the paving.

The key was still in his girdle bag. I held it up.

"Hurry! There's not a moment to lose." She grabbed my hand, and without looking back, we ran past the statue of Anubis into the labyrinth.

Neither of us said Samut's name. Neither of us spoke.

We hurried away, my breath coming in huge gasps. The sound of our sandals slapping against the stone. The thought of light at the end of the labyrinth pulling us forward.

My body suddenly seemed heavy. My legs slowed down beneath me as if someone had tied stones to them. I stopped and saw Isikara had stopped as well. She stared back at me.

The deep, dark well behind us was pulling us back.

What? What are you looking at? I wanted to yell at her.

But we stood there, arms at our sides, each with our own thoughts swirling around. Not looking at each other anymore. Facing forward to the light, with the darkness at our back.

The darkness and Samut splashing around and around in the oily black water.

He would get weaker and weaker. Sink into the water. First his mouth, then his nose, and lastly his eyes. Then nothing. Just the black oily water.

We can't, is what I wanted to shout.

Isikara looked back at me. In the lamplight a shadow seemed to pass over her face. Without speaking we both turned. Started walking back. Then, running. Isikara, pulling me along so that our breath came in gasps again.

At the edge of the well I squeezed my eyes shut. Hung back. Folded myself into the darkness. Held my breath. He had surely drowned already.

But I heard a faint splash. He was still alive.

"Samut!" I heard Isikara call. "Keep swimming, Samut! We'll be back soon." Then she turned to me. "Quick!" She crossed onto the stone slab that lay across the well's opening and held the lamp up high.

"Come on, Ta-Miu!"

I stared down at the water as I stepped onto the narrow slab and tried to force my feet forward. Far below I could see Samut's face staring up, as pale as a moon in the darkness. How cold the water must be. How cold would it be to sink under it forever?

"Step across, Ta-Miu! You *have* to! Stop looking down. Look at me." She held her hand out and grabbed me as I collapsed against her. "Quick!" She pulled me down some steps into a long passage that led into a vast chamber with a ceiling that disappeared into darkness. In the middle of the vault was a huge stone sarcophagus . . . King Amenhotep's, surely.

There was no time to get my bearings. Isikara pulled me into a side chamber. In the lamplight everything glittered. Heaps of chariots lay piled in a corner. Statues of gold stared back. Caskets lay open, with jewels scattered across the floor.

"Where are we?" My voice came out in a strange, hoarse whisper.

"King Amenhotep's storage chamber for his afterlife." She started pulling things, flinging open caskets and rummaging. "Find any length of material that's strong. There must be something we can use. Pray that Samut knocked out those guards well enough and they don't come around too soon. And pray Samut manages to keep swimming."

"What are we going to do?"

"Pull him up, of course!" She grabbed a bundle of cloth stacked up in a far corner. "Here. Take a few. We might have to tie them together. Hurry!"

I stood looking at her. "Why?"

"Why what?"

"Why're you doing this? Why are you rescuing him? Samut murdered the person you loved."

Isikara twitched her shoulders as if something prickly had fallen down her back. "We have to do what's right."

I could hear Samut's splashes even before we reached the well.

"Praise Hathor," Isikara breathed. "He's still alive." She called down, "Samut! We've got a cloth. We're going to pull you up." She grabbed a length and tied a knot around the head of the statue of Anubis. "That'll anchor him in case we slip."

Slip? Might we slip? My heart thumped in my throat as I peered down into the well.

Isikara hurled the other end of the cloth into the well. "A pestilence! It doesn't reach. Quick. Hand me another length," she said as she pulled it back up.

My hands were shaking as I tied a knot to join the two pieces. The guard right next to us was rolling his eyes and moaning. It looked as if he might come around at any moment.

We could have gone. We might have made it in time. We could have run for the labyrinth gate. Escaped. Just the two of us. Isikara and I. Isikara had escaped this tomb once already. With Tuthmosis.

Now she would escape it with his murderer.

She was ripping off her sandals. She nodded. "Take yours off as well. To give more grip."

She flung the end of the cloth down. "Can you reach it? Are you ready, Samut?" Her voice echoed into the well. "Put your feet against the sides as we pull. Find any ridge to give you grip," Isikara shouted.

She nodded at me. I crouched down in front with her at my back. My shoulders felt as if they were ripping from my flesh as we took the full burden of him. I felt my feet losing their footing. Slipping forward. *Please, Horus, don't let the cloth rip. Don't let us be dragged in.*

We could hear Samut grunting with his efforts.

"Step back from the edge, Ta-Miu!" Isikara shouted close to my ear. "You'll fall in!"

I looked down. My feet were just a pace away from the edge. I pulled with all my strength. Suddenly I saw Samut's hand.

"Help him while I keep holding," I cried.

Then there were two hands on the edge and his face appeared, his legs scrabbling against the rock while I tried to get a grip of slippery shoulders and ease him over onto the paving.

For a moment our eyes locked. Then he gripped

my hand and fell forward at my feet. Wet. Slimy. Exhausted.

"Quick now, Samut." Isikara reached down to help. "There's no time. We have to run for it. You knocked out the guards but they'll recover soon."

Samut shook his head. No life left in his eyes. "There's no point."

"What?"

"What's the point of me coming with you? I'll meet my end in any case. I'm doomed if I return. And doomed if I stay locked in here."

Isikara tried to urge him up. "Stop wasting time. Come on!"

I looked across at him, suddenly annoyed. "Do you think we did all this so we could have you arrested and put to death?"

"Why else?"

"Why would we risk our lives to save you? We could've escaped easily."

"Come now, Samut," Isikara said briskly. "You have to speak out against Wosret. That'll be your protection. And the fact that you stood by us with these guards. You have my word."

We all three stumbled forward through the

labyrinth. Stumbled out of the dark passages into the shining light of Thebes.

The sun blazed down and blinded our eyes. The great chalky cliff rose up behind us, and the green valley with the wide river below shivered in brightness. Shimmered and glimmered as never before.

We were free.

Who would've believed we could feel such happiness? The mud and slime dried and cracked against our skins. We looked at one another and laughed. And gasped huge gulps of air.

We had never known such light, such air, such perfume, such freedom as that afternoon as we ran through the fields of Thebes away from the darkness of the tomb.

Epilogue

✦ ✕ ✦ ✕ ✦ ✕ ✦ ✕ ✦

We entered the Great Hall with the muck of the labyrinth still stuck to us. We stood there in the stone doorway covered in mud and slime.

All eyes turned toward us, as if we were creatures who'd crawled back from the afterlife.

They had believed us dead. But now we were walking forward . . . Isikara, Samut, and I . . . our feet leaving muddy prints on the pattern of herons and lotus lilies that floated across the tiled floor.

We were real! We were alive! As alive as any of them standing there gawping.

It was Isikara who spoke first. Even then her voice was firm. She bowed and addressed Amenhotep and Nefertiti. "We've escaped the labyrinth. We've brought Samut back as well."

She said no more, but I knew it was Wosret that her words were meant for. She was challenging him to speak.

All eyes turned to him. But for once the silence held. Wosret's words dried up in the back of his throat.

Isikara urged Samut forward. "We brought him back so justice can be done. Listen to his story, and you will know where the real evil lies."

Then Nefertiti and Amenhotep heard the true story of all that had happened, from the time of Tuthmosis's chariot accident to the time of Wosret trying to poison Tuthmosis, and finally to the time of Tuthmosis's death.

The truth was told. And justice was done.

Thebes was deserted and rebuilt farther north along the Great River at the new city of Amarna. The Priests of Amun lost their power to the sun god Aten. There in the splendor of Amarna, with all its art and beauty, Amenhotep ruled as king, unchallenged until his death. He changed his name from Amenhotep to Akhenaten to show his love of Aten. And Nefertiti's first child was born. A daughter named Meritaten.

After that she bore five more beautiful daughters. But never a son.

At Amarna, Isikara became a high priestess of Aten, the god of light, and was no longer haunted by the image of the great crocodile god, Sobek, rising up to tear her apart. And in Amarna, Samut was reinstated at the new stables, with the magnificent chariot racing arena, where he became the best horse trainer ever known in the kingdom of Egypt.

And there Ta-Miu, true to her family heritage, employed all the skills she had learned from her father and brothers in Mitanni and worked side by side next to Samut. She was the first woman ever to be employed in the royal stables, but not the first woman to drive her own chariot!

And in Amarna, Kiya grew more and more radiant . . . so radiant that Amenhotep, now called Akhenaten, had a sun court built especially for her. And a small ripple passed through the peace of the new palace when Kiya bore him a son.

His *only* son. The son's name was Tutankhaten.

Tutankhaten renamed himself Tutankhamun, after the old god Amun. He died young and was buried with six chariots and many treasures and caskets of jewels. And he lay, silent and undisturbed, in his gold death mask and gold mummy case under the Theban mountains for thousands of years, until his tomb was finally discovered.

As for Wosret? The history of Wosret is unrecorded. He disappeared. Some say he was made to drink poison that same day in the Great Hall. Some say the cheetahs were allowed to take their revenge. Others say his death was devised by Nefertiti, that she had him thrown to the sacred crocodiles at the Temple of Sobek. And in so doing, she condemned him to the worst death of all. A death where nothing remained to be mummified, so his spirit could never be reunited with his body in the afterlife.

But whatever end came to him, it's clear that his

name was erased from the history of Egypt. No sign will be found of him, or his name, on any building, amulet, or wig box, and no statue will be found, even toppled in the desert sand, nor any mummy buried deep in the labyrinth of the chalk mountains of Thebes.

The labyrinths have been the resting places for mummies of kings and commoners, and creatures—from bulls to baboons and from crocodiles to cats—for thousands of years.

And somewhere out in the sands of the desert, there is even said to be a lion burial ground in homage to the fighting spirit of the goddess Sekhmet . . . the Lady of Flame.

But no mummy will *ever* be found of Wosret.

Justice was done.

ABOUT THE AUTHOR

Dianne Hofmeyr grew up next to the sea on the southern tip of Africa. Her travels with notebook and camera to Egypt, Tunisia, and Senegal; through China and Vietnam; and across Siberia have led to stories that have won South Africa's M-Net Book Prize, the Sanlam Gold for Youth Literature, and the Young Africa Award, and have twice been named IBBY Honour Books. She is also the author of *Fish Notes and Star Songs* and several picture books based on Ancient Egyptian myths. Visit her at www.diannehofmeyr.com.

Can one girl make eleven
wishes come true?

Enter a magical new world from the
bestselling author of

THE VAMPIRE DIARIES
AND
NIGHT WORLD

L. J. SMITH

FROM ALADDIN
Published by Simon & Schuster

THE 13TH REALITY

JAMES DASHNER

What if every choice you made created a new, alternate reality?
What if those realities were in danger and it was up to you to save them?
Would you have the courage?

FROM ALADDIN / PUBLISHED BY SIMON & SCHUSTER